A SLIPPERY SLOPE

A Clowder Cats Cozy Mystery Book #2

COURTNEY MCFARLIN

Chapter One

My boots crunched through the snow as I walked from my cabin to the main office of the resort, gripping my coat around my neck to keep the cold air out. A slight glow in the east told me the sun was on its way, but right now, it was pitch black and colder than I would've thought possible. Even though the walk was short, every step made me miss my warm bed and the cat, Jasper, currently snuggled into it.

Jasper was continuing to improve, but that also meant he was making noise about returning to his clowder in the woods. Luckily, this cold snap had convinced him to extend his stay with me. I wasn't sure what I'd do once it broke, but right now, since it was supposed to last for at least another week, I had more pressing worries.

I wrapped my mittened hand around the door handle and pulled, racing into the welcome warmth of the lobby. I'd expected it to be quiet, given that it was just a little after six, but a flurry of activity met my eyes. My new friend, Charlie, waved as she popped up from behind the front desk.

"Eden! There you are. Just in time. We need to get the ballroom ready for tonight and we're short on help."

That's me, Eden Brooks. My first name's Shireen, but since I'd never liked the name I'd been saddled with, I switched to my middle name when I started my job, and my new life, here at the Valewood Resort a few weeks ago. I was still getting used to the switch, in more ways than one. I unwound my scarf and smiled at Charlie. Her brown hair was pulled up, revealing the bright cherry red dye on the bottom half. I'd just helped her touch it up, and my fingers were still stained.

"Hey, Charlie. What can I do to help?"

"We've got to stack the chairs and tables in the storage room and then set up the banquet tables on the side. The ski team should arrive in the next few hours and I know Mr. Marsburg wants everything ready, even though we won't be using the room until tonight."

She raced around the corner, cracking her gum, and motioned for me to follow her. I stopped for a second to hang my coat, hat, and scarf on the hooks near the desk before heading down the hall. I was still learning the ropes at the resort, and this was the first big event we'd hosted since I started.

"This seems like a huge deal," I said, panting with the effort of keeping up with my energetic friend.

"Oh, it's enormous. They stay with us every year, even though the nearest slopes are about a half hour away. The team captain's father and Mr. Marsburg go way back."

"I wondered about that. You'd think they would want to stay right on the slopes."

I caught up with Charlie right as she opened the double doors leading to the ballroom and walked in behind her. The gleaming wooden beams drew my eyes immediately upward. Thanks to the chaos that surrounded my arrival at the resort, I still hadn't done a full tour or explored the place. I'd been too busy learning how to become a PR manager and filling in where I was needed.

A vast bank of windows lined the side of the room, making the space feel ever bigger. The marble tiles on the floor probably cost more than my annual salary. My mouth fell open as I turned in a slow circle, taking it all in. This was the most luxurious room I'd ever been in, and that's saying a lot since I used to work for Ken

Brockman, one of Hollywood's elite actors, who unfortunately played the role of entitled jerk in real life. I stuffed those memories back down where they belonged and smiled as Danny walked past, carrying three chairs.

"Hey, Eden! Are you here to help, too?"

I nodded at Valewood's resident jokester and consumer of potatoes as he passed by. Danny wore several hats at the resort, serving as the valet parking, bellhop, and the doorman, and all the odd jobs in between.

"I am. Do I just need to put those chairs on the cart?"

"You got it," he said, flashing me a thumbs up with one hand as he balanced his load with the other.

The chairs tipped alarmingly, and he immediately righted them, averting disaster with a grin. Charlie rolled her eyes, and I followed her to the next table.

"We'll be sensible and carry them one at a time," she said. "How's Jasper?"

I picked up a chair and led the way over to the cart Danny had in the middle of the room. It was already almost full, and it took all of my strength to get my chair onto the top of the last stack.

"Better," I said, once I had it situated. "He's snuggling with me at night and he's eating well, putting on some much needed weight."

"I'm gonna take this to the storage room," Danny said, groaning theatrically as he pushed the cart past us. "Be right back."

Charlie waited for him to leave the room before turning to face me.

"And how are you?"

I shrugged and turned away, walking back to the table to grab another chair.

"I'm okay."

Charlie beat me back to the table and put her hands on the chair I was going to pick up, her head tilted to the side.

"Eden, someone tried to kill you. Someone who murdered a guest. It's okay to be a little rattled."

I focused on the long braid I wore over my shoulder to avoid meeting her eyes. Charlie meant well. She really did. And I knew she had a point. I was still having nightmares about running into Emma in the woods as she desperately tried to cover her tracks and escape after murdering Sherry Youngstown. I took a deep breath and let it all out in a gust.

"I'm fine. To be honest, I'm just sad that she felt she needed to go to those lengths to get justice. Have you heard anything about her?"

Charlie patted me on the shoulder and took the chair, talking over her shoulder as she walked back to the middle of the room.

"Mr. Marsburg is paying for her defense attorney. That's all I know. It's just so sad that she lost her mom and now she's going to lose her freedom for the foreseeable future."

"Exactly. What she did was awful and wrong, but gosh, the Youngstowns were just awful people."

Our former guests were slumlords who'd owned an apartment building where a fire killed several people. One of those people was Emma's mother. When she realized she'd been assigned to clean the room of the people who'd played a role in the horrible fire, she'd snapped and killed the wife in a fit of anger.

We were all still trying to put ourselves back together after she'd confessed to me, after trying to kill me to make sure I kept quiet. The sad thing was, I hadn't even suspected her until she'd told me herself. Unfortunately, I'd blamed the head of housekeeping, Penny, and we'd focused all of our attention on her. Penny was still, understandably, not a fan of me.

I shook off the gloom that threatened and forced a smile.

"That's great Mr. Marsburg is helping her. What else can you tell me about the ski team?"

Charlie walked by for the next chair, and the look she leveled at me told me she knew I was changing the subject on purpose.

"They come every year as part of their practice sessions before the big corporate sponsored competitions start. I think they came in second last year, so I'm sure they're going to be gunning for first. The captain, Rob, is pretty nice and his sister is, too. For a while, there was some gossip that his sister was going to marry Mr. Marsburg, but something happened, and they split up."

Danny came rumbling back into the room, pushing the now empty cart in front of him.

"Hey, you're both here gossiping while I'm busting my back," he said, dropping a wink in my direction. "Let's go, people."

"What were we supposed to do, genius? You had the cart. We can't make the chairs float out of here on their own."

"Yeah, yeah," Danny said. "Where's everybody else?"

We worked together as Charlie ran down everyone's assignments for the big event.

"Wendy's coming in later since she'll be here all day. Carl's working on getting the lot cleared of snow, which isn't easy since we're supposed to get another five inches today alone. Trevor and his security team are making sure everything's ready for all the expensive gear the team's bringing. Denise from HR is coming in early to help, and the kitchen staff is racing to get the spread ready for tonight's banquet."

Danny stacked a chair and rubbed his stomach.

"I sure hope they don't forget about us."

Charlie elbowed him in the side and shook her head.

"They never would. I think Denise said Mr. Marsburg is planning something special for us. She wouldn't tell me, though, and trust me, I tried to worm it out of her."

We focused on our work and before we knew it, everything had been cleared out of the ballroom. Danny left with the cart and we trailed after him to help him load the banquet tables back on to it. I stopped at the doorway of the ballroom, looking back at the expanse of polished floor. It looked even bigger now that was empty. I could imagine music playing while people danced.

"Hey, at least this place isn't the one that inspired The Shining," Charlie said, coming back to collect me. "I always think of that when I look at the ballroom."

She let out a dramatic shudder and made a face.

"The Shining?"

"Yeah, The Overlook at Estes. Wait, are you telling me you never saw that movie?"

I shook my head as we trailed after Danny. I'd been raised in an extremely strict household, one where books and movies were shunned and only narrow views were permitted. I'd grown up a voracious reader, but I'd steered clear of the horror genre, focusing instead on mysteries that I could sneak in without my mother noticing.

"Oh my gosh, girl. I know what we're doing on my next night off. Scary movie time! I'll have to see what streaming service has it. It's a classic."

I gave a noncommittal shrug, and we focused on loading up the heavy tables while she chattered on about her love of scary movies. Danny was also a fan and before I knew it, they were planning on bringing the rest of the staff who lived on site in for a shared movie night. I smiled as they grew more animated. I wasn't used to being surrounded by such friendly, open people, and I wouldn't knock it. If that meant I'd get my socks scared off, so be it.

"I'll make the popcorn," I said, jumping in.

"Yes! I'll find some movie candy and we'll make it an event," Charlie said, popping her gum.

We spent the next hour getting the banquet tables set up and by the time Denise walked in, everything was ready. She laughed as she stood in the doorway.

"Well, I picked a great time to show up. Come on, guys, Mr. Marsburg has a special announcement for all of us. We're supposed to gather in the lobby."

Charlie and I shared an excited look before following Denise down the hall. Danny pestered her to reveal the secret, but she mimed zipping her lips and forced us to wait. Once we were in the lobby, I spotted a sleepy-looking Wendy standing behind the desk and sent her a wave.

She yawned widely before returning it. My answering smile slid off my face as Penny turned and spotted me. As always, the head of housekeeping was impeccably dressed, her hair scraped back into the tightest bun imaginable. She looked down her nose at my casual outfit, chosen since I'd known we'd probably be doing manual labor, and sniffed, turning away.

My face reddened as Charlie snorted.

"I don't know why she's always got to be so unpleasant. It's got to be the bun. I can hear her hair follicles screaming from here."

I shushed my irrepressible friend and focused on Mr. Marsburg as he walked in, wreathed in smiles. Our boss was a handsome man who would've looked completely at home in a high-fashion magazine. I'd heard cooking used to be his passion before his dad put him in charge of the resort, but he easily could've been a model if he'd wanted to.

Penny snapped at the housekeeping staff and they quieted, turning to face our boss as Carl walked in, stomping the snow off his boots.

"Great, everyone's here," Mr. Marsburg said, still grinning. "I appreciate all the extra effort every one of you has put into getting this place ready for our special guests. As a way of saying thank you, I'd like to invite all of you to take part in tonight's welcome banquet."

Everyone started murmuring at once and a jolt of excitement was palpable. Danny held up a hand and Marsburg nodded..

"Yes, Danny, there will still be a breakfast service, and bagged lunches will be available for everyone. Dinner will be served at the banquet."

"Yeah!"

Danny pumped a fist in the air.

"I'll let you all get back to work, but thank you again. I look forward to seeing all of you tonight."

He nodded and headed back to his office, leaving us to mill around. Trevor, the head of security, walked over. His bearded face was all smiles.

"Eden, are you excited about the first big event? We've closed off all the bookings, so it will just be the team here for the next two weeks."

"I think so. I'm not sure I'll go to the banquet, but I appreciate Mr. Marsburg inviting us."

"Oh, you're coming," Charlie said, threading her arm through mine. "Don't even try to wiggle out of it. Let's go pick out what we're going to wear before breakfast."

"But..." I said, dragging my feet as she tried to haul me over to where our coats were hanging.

"Girl, I've already seen your closet. Don't worry, we're going to my cabin. I've got the perfect dress for you. And when we're done with that, we're having breakfast."

I glanced at Trevor helplessly.

"Don't resist. She's an unstoppable force. See you later, Eden. Don't expect me to save you any hash browns, Charlie."

Charlie made a rude noise before elbowing me in the side and giving me a pathetic pair of puppy dog eyes. There was no choice but to give in. I bundled up while Charlie rattled on about what she was going to do with my hair. Before I knew it, I was being led to her cabin, following the newly shoveled path Carl had made for us.

Chapter Two

An hour later, armed with a dress I still couldn't imagine myself wearing, and feeling as though I'd walked up a mountain, twice, I stumbled back to my cabin. Charlie was the best, but right now, I needed a little peace, especially after the chaos of breakfast at the dining hall. I needed Jasper. I paused, hand on my door, and listened for a second. A skittering sound was coming from within, a sound that made the corners of my mouth turn up.

I eased open the door and spotted Jasper batting a toy fish and then leaping after it as it shot across the floor. He was playing! He spotted me, golden eyes flaring in alarm, before he turned away, licking his thin side. He wasn't embarrassed, was he? I walked over to the closet to hang the dress.

"Hi Jasper. I see you're keeping your skills fresh. That's smart."

I turned back in time to see him nodding.

"Yes. I need to be sharp when I return to the clowder. I don't want to miss a step while I'm living in the lap of luxury."

I smiled at the thought of my tiny cabin being called the lap of luxury, but I supposed it was to a cat who'd lived most of his life outside. I flopped down on the bed and he joined me, making a creaky leap. I held my hand out to him and he butted it, purring deep within his chest.

Jasper wasn't a young cat. When I'd found him a few weeks ago, he'd been near the end, but thanks to the local vet, he was doing better. The last thing I wanted was for him to return to the woods, even though I know he missed his clowder. He'd lead them for years, keeping the cats and kittens safe. Fig, his second in command, was in charge now, and he seemed fine with it, as long as it was a temporary situation. I was determined that Jasper would stay with me, despite his protests. I thought I was wearing him down, but when he said things like that, I wasn't so sure.

"What's up at the office?" he asked, settling down for a bath.

While he spread his toes, delicately cleaning between them, I filled him in on the morning's events, still marveling that we could talk the way we did. I wasn't sure how, and I certainly didn't know why I'd suddenly developed the ability to talk to cats, but I wouldn't trade it for anything. An entirely new world had opened at my feet, and I was determined not to squander it.

It was an ability my friend, Hannah Murphy, shared. According to her, and the mysterious Anastasia Aspen, they'd hoped I'd be able to speak to cats as they could, and take care of the clowder. It had been a few days since I'd talked to Hannah and I wondered what she, and her adorable crew of cats, were up to.

"So people pay good money to go out in the cold and hurtle down mountains?" Jasper asked, breaking into my thoughts.

I hadn't realized I'd trailed off, content to sit in silence, listening to the soothing sounds of Jasper bathing until he spoke.

"They do. I've never done it, but I've seen it on television. It looks like it might be fun."

"Humans. I don't know if I'll ever understand them," Jasper said, shaking his grizzled head.

"That makes two of us, Jasper."

I smoothed the fur between his ears and stood up. I needed to get back to work, but I wanted just a few more minutes with my furry friend.

"What's the plan for the rest of the day?"

I drummed my fingers on the countertop of my kitchenette, mentally organizing my tasks for the day before I answered.

"I need to work on my PR training. With everything that's happened, I feel like I've fallen behind. I'm caught up on my online schooling, but I wouldn't mind working ahead. That's what I was going to do until this banquet thing came up."

Hannah had pulled some strings with her old professor and helped me get a spot in the university's online journalism program. I could go at my pace, which enabled me to work during the day, but I wanted to move forward as fast as I could. I loved learning, and I loved my new job, minus the whole murderous co-worker thing.

"Will you be back before the banquet starts?" Jasper asked, not making eye contact.

"Of course. I've got to make sure you get plenty to eat. I may even grab a few little treats for you from the buffet. And don't worry, I'll make sure the clowder gets their food tonight. I know Luke's going to be busy, but he'd never forget the cats."

Luke worked in the kitchens and before I'd been hired at the resort, he was the one who took care of the clowder, feeding them the leftovers from the resort every night. They trusted him, and ever since I'd started helping him, they were begrudgingly letting me in. Well, a little. I had a feeling Fig still had her doubts about me. I smiled at the thought of the cranky brown cat. She was one of a kind.

Jasper nodded, but I could see he was relieved.

"That's good. I've been worried about them with this cold snap," he said, staring out the snow encrusted window.

He wasn't the only one worried about the cats. I'd rounded up extra blankets as soon as I'd seen the forecast, and argued with Fig until she took them. She still wouldn't let me see where the cats slept, but at least she'd allowed me to leave the blankets for the cats to drag where they were needed.

"Fig will keep them safe and warm. One of us will check on them tonight," I said. "I'd better get back to work. Do you need anything?"

He shook his head and burrowed into the down comforter on

the bed. I cherished the victory I'd won, convincing him it was best for the clowder if he stayed healthy and avoided going back in the cold until he was one hundred percent healthy, but every day I dreaded him changing his mind. I quickly checked his food and water bowls before getting bundled back up for the quick trip to my office. I closed the door behind me, pinching my face as the frigid blast of air whistled down through the row of cabins.

I hustled back to the main building and stopped at the front desk, where Wendy was standing. The lobby had emptied, but there was still a hum of anticipation almost palpable in the air.

"Wendy, are you all set?" I asked, leaning against the counter.

"As ready as I'm going to be," she said, looking at her watch. "The team is supposed to arrive in two hours. I've gone over everything twice, and if I do it again, I'll worry about my sanity."

"This is an enormous deal, huh?"

She nodded, curls springing with the movement. I noticed she'd gone all out with her makeup and was wearing her nicest sweater. Its deep olive green color brought out the gold highlights in her eyes.

"It is. They're practically royalty in these parts. Their new coach, Christian St. John, is one of the premier skiers in the state. Twenty years ago, he brought home gold in the Alpine."

His name meant nothing to me, but from the flush spreading on Wendy's cheeks, she didn't feel the same way.

"Well, that sounds pretty impressive. I'd better hurry and try to get some work in before they show up. We're all supposed to gather here to greet them, right?"

"Yes, Mr. Marsburg wants them to be treated like family. It's a little ritual we've always done for the team."

"I'll be here. See you later, Wendy."

She nodded, clearly distracted, and checked her watch again. I had a feeling someone had a tiny crush on this ski coach. I headed back to my office, pausing when I heard my boss call my name. I poked my head into his office and he beckoned me in.

"How are you settling in, Eden?"

He leaned forward, elbows on his desk, and searched my eyes as

I sat down. I hadn't been here long, but I'd quickly learned he was an excellent boss. He truly cared about his employees and their happiness. Our salaries were more than generous and the included room and board were definitely appreciated.

"Just fine," I said, nodding. "I've got some ideas for some marketing campaigns we can run in the spring. I'm learning so much thanks to those courses you recommended."

"Great. I can't wait to see them," he said, his handsome face relaxing into a smile. "You're sure you're okay after what happened? If you need to take some time off, paid, of course, I completely understand."

I shook my head. Time off to be alone with my thoughts was the last thing I wanted. It may not be healthy, but I preferred to bury my head in my work.

"Thank you, I appreciate it, but I'm at my happiest working. I should have my presentation ready for you by the time the ski team checks out."

"There's no rush. The next few weeks are going to be intense. In past years, we always had the event catered, so this will be the first time the entire staff comes together. You've been so helpful, always filling in where you're needed. You've shown genuine talent and initiative, Eden, and it's appreciated. The PR stuff can wait."

I was still amazed I'd landed a boss who wasn't concerned that I was earning every penny of my salary doing the job I was hired to do. I sent a silent thank you to Hannah for landing me this job as I stood.

"Well, I'll be out front with the welcome wagon when they arrive. Just let me know if there's anything I can do in the meantime."

"Thanks, Eden."

He turned back to his computer, and I walked the short distance to my office, flipping on the light. It was a tiny space, but it was all mine, and it even had a window that looked out over the mountains, even if the view was obscured today. I'd come a long way from my job at the Brockman estate.

I fired up my computer, flipping between another PR course,

and the presentation I'd mentioned to my boss. I was new to a lot of these tasks, but I'd been surprised at how much I enjoyed it. The minutes flew and before I knew it, the growing buzz coming from the lobby told me I needed to wrap it up for the day and join my coworkers.

I shut everything down, grabbed my bag, and headed for the front. Charlie was there, waving madly, looking none the worse for wear even though she'd worked all night and probably was running on two hours of sleep, max. I slipped next to her and turned to look outside in time to see a shiny, enormous bus roll into the parking lot.

"They're here," Charlie squealed, jumping in place.

The door opened, and I craned my head to see the ski team as they came down the steps, caught up in the excitement everyone else was feeling. Danny opened the doors, ushering them inside, where everyone was lined up. The handsome man in the lead looked to be in his forties, and from the nervous expression on Wendy's face, he had to be Christian St. John. He walked down the line, shaking everyone's hand. By the time he got to me, I could feel Wendy's nervousness. I smiled, shook his hand, and turned to Wendy.

"This is Wendy, Mr. St. John. She's our resident miracle worker at the front desk."

Wendy shot me a grateful smile before focusing on the man in front of her. His eyes crinkled as he nodded.

"Wonderful. One never knows when one will need a miracle."

She nodded, her expression worshipful, as he winked, before continuing down the line. I turned to smile at the man in front of me. His lips quirked as he watched his coach.

"Nice to meet you. I'm Rob Yardley, team captain. This is my sister, Rebecca."

"Eden? What a beautiful name," Rebecca said, her smile genuine. "It's nice to meet you."

The rest of the team was a blur as names were exchanged and they moved down the line. Wendy rushed behind the desk and handed out all the keycards. Danny and Penny offered to lead everyone to their rooms, and the noise level finally dropped off as everyone left the lobby.

"Wasn't Jude dreamy?" she asked, her eyes sparkling.

"Which one was he?"

"The tall blond with the gorgeous smile."

Ah. He was the one who'd seemed sincere, but his handshake felt smarmy. I wasn't about to contradict my friend, though.

"He was nice. Who was the other one?"

"Troy Lawton. He's been with the team forever. He's a pain. Jude must be new."

"The girls were nice," I said, casting about for something to say. "They're all so tall."

"Watch out for Sassy. She comes off all pleasant, but she's anything but. Alicia is new. She's so young."

I nodded. The youngest team member, Alicia Davenport, had struck me as being as overwhelmed as I was, especially when her wary eyes met mine. I made a mental note to make sure she felt at home. She looked about seventeen, and I couldn't imagine dealing with all of this at such a young age.

"Thanks for the warning. What do we do now?"

Charlie yawned and stretched.

"I don't know about you, but I'm going back to bed. I'll pop by your cabin to do your hair before the banquet. Laters!"

She waved, leaving me in the lobby, playing nervously with my braid. I'd done nothing like this before and suddenly, the thought of going to the banquet seemed a little much. I headed back to my office, determined to get some more work done before the big event.

Chapter Three

I looked into the full-length mirror in Charlie's cabin and for a second, my brain didn't comprehend the image in front of me. Who was this person in the mirror? It sort of looked like me, but not a version I'd ever seen before. I turned to Charlie, where she was waiting, hands clasped, bouncing in place.

"I love it. I don't know how you did that with my hair, and I'm certain I'll never be able to replicate it, but it's amazing."

I looked back into the mirror and shook my head. My long, waist length hair looked like it belonged to a fairy princess, not boring old Eden Brooks. Charlie braided sections, curled the rest, and I didn't dare touch it in fear of it all unraveling.

Charlie squealed and grabbed for her makeup bag.

"I'm so happy you like it. Ever since I saw your hair down, I knew I had to do something that would do it justice. Now, for makeup, I'm thinking of something very simple."

Considering Charlie's eye shadow matched the vibrant cherry red under dye on her hair, I wasn't sure what that meant, but I let her work her magic. I certainly had no clue what I was doing, and if how she looked tonight was any sign, Charlie Turner was a master. I closed my eyes and trusted the process.

"There," Charlie said, stepping back with a nod after just a few minutes. "Perfection."

I slowly opened my eyes, and a smile crept across my face. Just a soft feathering of glittery eyeshadow, a little mascara and lip gloss. This was something I could replicate.

"I love it."

I gave her a hug, squeezing her extra tight until she squealed and jumped back.

"No wrinkles or creases. I want everyone to see how beautiful you are."

It felt like a shame to put my down jacket over my dress, but there was no way we were walking to the lodge building without them. Charlie put a few finishing touches on her makeup while I shrugged into my coat and put on my boots for the short walk.

"Are you sure you don't want to wear these heels?" she asked, dangling a pair from her fingers.

I shook my head and held up my pair of black flats before stuffing them in my pockets.

"No, I'd end up in a heap."

"Don't sell yourself short. I'm going to risk it. It's one of the few times a year we get to get dressed up here and I'm going to take full advantage of it. Besides, did you see how tall some of those skiers are?"

We laughed as we headed outside, braced against the cold. I put my hand on her arm, slowing her steps.

"Charlie, you don't know what this means to me. I never got to go to prom or do anything like this before. I always dreamt of having a best friend like you. Thank you."

Her eyes went misty, and she shook her finger at me.

"No. I did not spend twenty minutes getting this cat eye liner perfect to cry now. It's freezing out here. Let's make a run for it."

I glanced back towards my cabin, wondering how Jasper was. We had our nightly routine of snuggling on the bed while I did my coursework and I was missing him.

"Come on, Eden!"

I turned and hurried into the building, holding up my face as the warm air from the lobby heater blasted me. The lobby lights were low and I could hear music coming from the ballroom. I followed Charlie behind the desk and we hung up our coats and slipped into our nice shoes. She grabbed my hand before I could walk down the hall and looked me up and down.

"Still perfect. I knew teal would work for you. It's never done me any favors. That's your dress, now."

I smoothed the silky fabric down my hips and shook my head.

"Charlie, I couldn't. This must have cost a fortune. And you would look good wearing a bag."

"Whatever. It made me look positively bilious. I just wish Ethan could see you tonight. Have you heard from him after he arrested Emma?"

She fussed with her dress, knowing full well she'd just dropped a verbal bomb. Luckily, there was no way I was going to run into Valewood's police detective tonight. Even though Ethan Rhodes was one of the handsomest men I'd ever met, I still wasn't over an argument we'd had. He'd left a few messages, which I'd ignored, and that was fine with me. I wasn't ready to face him yet, and I wasn't sure I'd ever be ready.

"Let's go see what's going on in the ballroom. I can't wait to see everyone dressed up."

Being the good friend she was, Charlie let me evade her line of questioning and led the way to the ballroom. The chandeliers sparkled overhead as we entered. The tables we'd arranged earlier were groaning under the weight of the food the kitchen staff prepared, and everyone was milling around. I blinked, surprised at the amount of people inside the room and tugged on Charlie's arm.

"I thought it was just us and the ski team?"

She waved to Danny before leaning closer.

"I think some locals are here, too. This is a big deal. Hey, Danny. You cleaned up all right."

Danny rolled shoulders self consciously, and I patted his arm.

"You look great. That's a very nice shirt."

He flushed and stammered, not meeting my eyes.

"You look amazing, Eden. Charlie, you look okay, too."

She narrowed her eyes before he cackled with glee and she punched him on the arm. I watched the two of them interact and wondered if they'd ever be more than friends. Neither of them seemed to realize the tension that radiated everywhere when they were together. Happily, that was something to think about down the road. Tonight, I just wanted to take all of this in. A familiar voice sounded behind him.

"Eden! I want you to meet my wife. Eden, this is Annie."

I turned and spotted Trevor, who looked like a bear crammed into an uncomfortable suit, and his tiny wife. She was so ethereally delicate I felt like a moose as I shook her hand.

"It's nice to meet you, Annie. Trevor talks about you all the time."

She placed one of her small hands on his chest and threw back her head, unleashing a laugh that seemed way out-of-place coming out of that tiny body.

"You poor thing. Are you settling in here okay?"

I was drawn to her instant warmth and nodded, glancing up at Trevor to take in his giant beam of happiness.

"I am, thank you."

"How are the courses going?" Trevor asked.

Annie swatted at his arm and shook her finger at him.

"No shop talk. Come on, Eden. Let's go see what's at the buffet before all the good stuff is taken."

I glanced over my shoulder, but Charlie and Danny were deep in a heated argument about who knew what, and I figured eating was better than listening to those two. Besides, once they hit the table, Annie was right. All the good stuff would be gone. I followed in her wake, listening as she filled me in on everyone who was milling around.

"That's Diane Yardley. She's Rob and Rebecca's mom. They live the next town over, but she's always involved in local charity events. She's with the junior league, you know."

I didn't know, but Diane was a beautiful woman. Her snow white hair was styled in a perfect bob and her silver dress sparkled under the lights. She had her head bent, listening to another woman I didn't recognize.

"Who's that?"

Annie stood on her tiptoes to peer over my shoulder.

"Oh, that's Cecily Lawton. She's Troy's mother. She's been frenemies with Diane for years. You know the type, nice in public, but ready to tear each other's hair out at a moment's notice. Cecily's husband, Wilson, is over there."

I followed in the direction she was pointing and nodded politely. There were just too many unfamiliar people. I took the plate Annie handed me and followed as she filled her plate with many delicacies. I looked up and spotted a familiar face behind the table.

"Luke! It's good to see you. You guys did an amazing job tonight. The food looks incredible."

Luke nodded, his bony face breaking into a grin as his hazel eyes lit up.

"Thanks, Eden. Don't worry, I already fed the cats tonight. They're snug as bugs in rugs with plenty of treats to keep them warm. I took their meat in an insulated container, so it was nice and warm for them."

Relief flooded through me. I'd miss seeing the cats tonight, but knowing they'd had a good meal put me at ease.

"Thank you, Luke. That was very thoughtful."

"That's right. Trevor told me you two take care of the local clowder of cats. You know, that's something to ask Diane about. She could help organize a fund to help cover veterinarian expenses."

I perked up. I hadn't broached the subject with Jasper, or Fig, but it had been on mind. Getting the cats vaccinated, as well as fixed, was crucial.

"That would be amazing. I wouldn't know how to approach her, though."

"Leave that to me," Annie said, setting her pointy chin. "I work in her office. She's a lawyer. I'll ask her."

Ah, that's how she knew so much about the people at the banquet. I waved to Luke as we continued down the line and by the time we were done, I wasn't sure how Annie was carrying her loaded down plate.

She spotted me eyeing it and let out another surprising laugh.

"This isn't all for me. Most of it is for Trevor. Oh, look, here comes James."

I turned to see my boss, as he bowed slightly.

"Ladies. You both look lovely. I'm glad Trevor got you out of the house. It's been a while since you've joined us for an event."

"Aren't you cold?" Annie asked, her eyes narrow. "You were outside with Rebecca for quite a while."

Mr. Marsburg's handsome face flushed, and he glanced over his shoulder briefly.

"It was just a few minutes. Eden, if you'll excuse me?"

I nodded, surprised at his abruptness, and watched as he exited the room. Annie leaned closer.

"Well, it doesn't look like they're going to be getting back together. I had such hopes for them. They make a beautiful couple, even though he's so much older than Rebecca. Did you know they were briefly engaged?"

Add that to the long list of things I didn't know. I lost my boss in the crowd and turned back to Annie.

"I didn't. Shall we rejoin Trevor?"

I needed to get back to my comfort zone and out of the crush of people who were crowding the banquet tables. I headed for the edge of the room where I'd last seen Charlie, walking faster than Annie. I took a deep breath and slowed my steps, waiting for her to catch up.

She gave me a quick glance and freed a hand to pat my arm, almost upsetting her plate.

"It's okay, crowds can bother me, too. There's my handsome man."

She smiled up at Trevor as he leaned down to kiss her cheek, taking the overloaded plate off her hands.

"Thanks for making sure I didn't starve."

She patted his middle and shook her head.

"I don't think we have anything to worry about. Have you seen Charlie?"

Trevor looked behind him and pointed.

"She's over there, with Wendy and Denise."

I said my goodbyes to the couple and hustled over to Charlie. She was holding a flute of champagne and laughing at something Denise said as I approached.

"There you are. Ooo, you brought nibbles," she said, helping herself to a small pastry from my plate.

I didn't mind. My stomach was too busy tying itself into knots to think about eating. I handed the plate around to Wendy and Denise and focused back on the ballroom.

"Doesn't he look incredible?" Wendy asked.

I already knew who she meant by her sigh and looked around the room until I spotted Christian St. John. I could see why he made Wendy's heart flutter as he focused on the woman he was talking to. His tanned face contrasted nicely with his bright white shirt and black coat.

I turned to answer her when a scream rang out through the room, making me jump.

"She's dead! Rebecca's dead! I just found her on the balcony. Come quickly!"

I didn't recognize the woman's voice, but she sounded like she was around our age. I craned my head, trying to see who she was.

A second of stunned silence was broken as everyone began talking at the same time. A shriek went up from the last place I'd seen Diane Yardley. I looked around in time to see my boss, his face drained of color. He looked towards the ballroom doors and made a move towards them, before shaking his head and walking towards the crowd, head down.

The sound of a plate breaking made me jump again before I realized I'd dropped what I was holding. I knelt and began picking up the shattered pieces from the marble floor as blood pounded in my ears. Charlie joined me, her voice low.

"Eden? What's wrong?"

"Annie just said Mr. Marsburg was outside with Rebecca for a long time. Did you see how he reacted just now?"

She looked around the room and shook her head.

"I didn't. You don't think?"

I shook my head hard, and one of my small braids nearly whipped me in the face.

"He couldn't. Could he?"

Danny appeared, holding a bag, and helped us clean up the mess I'd made. Suddenly, Mr. Marsburg's voice rang out.

"Everyone, please stay put. I'm very sorry, but we've called the police and they'll be here shortly."

Loud voices filled the ballroom as I glanced helplessly at Charlie. I couldn't believe this was happening again.

Chapter Four

A s we waited for the police to arrive, the class divisions in the room were once again apparent. Instead of mingling as one, strict lines appeared to have been drawn in the sand. The ski team, minus Rob, huddled together, whispering and glancing over at us with suspicion in their eyes. Their parents and the other wealthy team supporters circled around Rebecca's parents, closing them off from view. That left us, the resort staff, off to one side, miserably trying to figure out what to do.

Mr. Marsburg appeared to be stuck somewhere in the middle. My eyes tracked him as he parted the people standing around the Yardleys, kneeling next to Diane, talking with them, while I attempted to ignore the worry twisting my stomach into knots.

The resort staff, myself included, were silent as we bunched together. Even Annie had nothing to say, her eyes huge in her face as she gripped Trevor's arm. The switch from a magical evening spent rubbing elbows with minor celebrities had twisted into something dark. I couldn't help but think of Rebecca and the sweet smile she'd given me just a few hours ago. Was she truly dead? Had there been some terrible mistake?

"Eden, he's here," Charlie said, her voice low and strained.

Her words pulled me back to reality, and I heard the sirens.I turned and winced as I immediately made brief eye contact with Ethan Rhodes. His freckled, honest face looked cast in stone, and his sky-blue eyes were hard as they scanned the room, assessing.

"Ladies and gentlemen, I'm Ethan Rhodes, with the Valewood Police Department."

A murmur went through the crowd and Marsburg stood. He nodded towards Ethan, and the crowd parted to let him through.

"Detective Rhodes, we appreciate you arriving so swiftly. If you'll follow me, I'll show you where the body is," he said, stumbling over his words. "Where Miss Yardley was found. We thought it best to leave her so as not to disturb the scene."

He was stiffly formal and his face tinged with gray as Ethan scanned the room.

"Thank you. Ladies and gentlemen," he said again. "I know you've experienced a terrible shock tonight, and would like nothing more than to go home, but I'll ask for your patience while we begin our investigation. If you could make yourselves comfortable, myself and my colleagues will interview with each of you."

Agreements filtered from around the room as Ethan followed Marsburg outside. Uniformed police officers came into the room and our little group pulled closer together. Trevor spoke quietly into his phone and I drifted closer, hoping to pick up the conversation.

"Josh, what's going on back there?"

Luckily, I could hear Josh's bluff voice through the phone as he answered.

"I'm sitting here minding my own business while you're rubbing elbows with the rich and famous. Is there any food left from the buffet?"

Trevor's face resembled a thundercloud as he pivoted towards the wall, walking away from me, and effectively cutting off Josh's voice.

"Have you been monitoring the feeds? Pull the cam feed from number twelve and do it now. There's been an incident."

I quickly put it together and relaxed a little. Obviously, there was a security camera that covered the patio. However Rebecca died, the event must have been captured. We'd know shortly if she'd been killed.

Charlie shifted her feet, winced, and looked around before putting her hand on my shoulder to balance herself while she slipped off her high heels.

"The one time I decide to wear these dang things," she muttered as she looped the straps over her fingers. "Oh, that's better."

Her toes curled against the cold of the marble floor as she looked around the room and leaned closer to me.

"Who did it? Someone on the ski team wanting to take her spot? Were the alternates here? I didn't see them."

"Alternates?" I asked, perking up.

"Yeah, the team has six people on it, but if one of them gets injured, they have to have someone to take their place. Usually, two or three alternates travel with the team, but they weren't on the bus this afternoon. Or if they were, I guess I didn't see them during the big welcome celebration."

I looked around the room and shrugged, but I liked the angle she was taking. I didn't want to think about Rebecca being murdered, but it made more sense that someone who had something to gain killed her, rather than our boss. Anybody but our boss.

A uniformed police officer approached our group, notebook at the ready, and we quieted. Trevor moved to the front, sliding his phone into his suit pocket.

"I'm Trevor Kent, the head of security," he said, taking charge. "Josh, one of my associates, is pulling the security footage from the outside cameras and will have it available for you shortly, officer."

The man in front of us relaxed and smiled, putting his hands on his hips.

"Great, great. I'm Officer Jenkins. I'll need to speak with each one of you. Mr. Kent, would you like to go first? I'll need the rest of you to stand over there, please," he said, pointing to a spot a few feet distant.

"They're separating us to ensure we don't discuss things too much and try to cover for one another. We've all got to get our stories straight."

Charlie rolled her eyes and poked Danny in the side.

"Somebody's been streaming too many cop shows. None of us are guilty, silly. Our stories are already straight."

Danny looked around the room, nodding towards the cluster of donors and parents.

"I think one of them did it. Did you hear Rebecca was going to announce her engagement?"

Wendy leaned closer, her face flushed.

"No! Who?"

"I dunno," Danny said, shrugging. "Some rich dude. I think he's over there next to her parents."

I marveled at everyone's ability to absorb gossip and glanced over at the cluster of people comforting the Yardley's. A tall man with dark hair kept glancing towards the patio. I didn't know his name, but that must be the fiance. Hmmm. He didn't look particularly upset, but I knew everyone processed grief differently. I shook my head and focused back on Wendy and Danny's conversation. The police were here, and they'd be the ones to solve this case, not me.

I missed part of what they were saying and they stopped talking as paramedics entered the ballroom, pushing a gurney. Their steps weren't hurried, and my stomach sank as the realization finally sunk in. Rebecca was truly dead, not just injured, and someone in this room was most likely the killer. I followed their progress through the room and spotted Marsburg standing next to Ethan, his arms folded over his chest.

Ethan held the doors open for the crew as they went outside and began lifting Rebecca's body onto the gurney. I turned away, not wanting to see. Charlie's face was pale as she stood on her tiptoes to see past me.

The room was so silent you could hear the rustle of the body bag. My stomach clenched painfully as someone touched my arm.

"Miss?"

I turned to face Officer Jenkins and nodded.

"Yes?"

"If I could have your statement?"

"Sure. I'm sorry. What do you need to know?"

"Could you detail your movements starting before the banquet until the victim was discovered?"

I listed out everything I'd done, but when I got to the part about seeing Marsburg with Annie, I stumbled. Officer Jenkins raised an eyebrow as I trailed off. I knew in my heart I had to do what was right, but I just hoped I wasn't throwing my boss under the bus.

"Mr. Marsburg said he'd been outside with Rebecca for just a few minutes," I said. "After that, we took our food over here and I was talking with my friends when someone shouted that Rebecca was dead."

He clicked his pen and nodded before turning to Charlie. Wendy grabbed my arm and hauled me backwards.

"Did you say Mr. Marsburg was outside with Rebecca before she was killed?" Wendy asked, whispering and looking around me towards the officer.

"I did. I had to be honest. He was only with her for a few minutes. I'm sure it will be fine."

"But what if?"

I gripped her upper arm and shook my head sharply.

"I don't believe he'd do anything to harm someone. He's the nicest boss I've ever had, and he's honest. He's not a killer."

"Eden, you don't know their history. After what Danny said, I could see Mr. Marsburg losing his cool. Rebecca ended their engagement when she made the ski team. She said she wasn't ready to settle down, and now, a year later, she's getting married to someone else? That's a slap in the face."

I paled as her words sunk in, but I still couldn't believe our boss killed a woman. He didn't have it in him. At least, not that I could see. I searched the room until I found him. He was squared off with the younger man Danny pointed out earlier, and from the looks on their faces, they weren't having a friendly conversation. Doubt pricked my spine.

"I don't know what to think, Wendy."

I moved towards the wall, desperate to get out of the crush of people milling around. All I wanted to do was go back to my cabin and crawl into bed, but there was no telling when we'd be able to leave. My feet carried me closer to the windows, and I spotted Ethan kneeling in the snow next to the patio. Had he found something?

A flash of movement caught my eye and my breath caught as I saw a cat, a few hundred yards from where Ethan was, its tail held high. Hope flared brightly. The cat was too far away to identify, but it could be a member of the clowder living in the woods. Had they seen something? I itched for a chance to get away and go talk with them.

The cat lashed its tail before bounding away through the snow, towards the woods. I put a hand on the window as it disappeared into the trees.

"Eden."

I turned and faced Ethan Rhodes as my stomach dropped. His cheeks and nose were flushed from the cold. His hair had grown a little since we'd last seen each other, as he took Emma from my cabin to book her for the murder of Sherry Youngstown. Had it really only been a few weeks?

"Ethan," I said, once I realized I'd been standing there, silently staring at him like a loon. "How... I mean, did you find anything out there? Any clues?"

He cocked his head to the side, seeming to weigh something, before letting out a breath and nodding.

"I found a ring in the snow. I need to see if it belonged to the victim. Are you?" he asked, trailing off and shaking his head. "Did you observe anything before the victim was found?"

"No, I'm sorry. I was getting some food at the banquet tables over there. I wasn't looking outside. Did she... did Rebecca suffer? She was so nice."

He let out a weary sigh and crossed his arms over his chest.

"It appears she was strangled, but the medical examiner will tell us more."

"It had to be someone in this room who killed her, didn't it?" I asked, looking around the room.

"There's always the possibility someone knew of the event

happening tonight and they were outside. I've tossed around the theory that it was a robbery gone wrong, but I saw no footprints leading away from the scene. I think it is probable it was someone here."

"The ring. Was it an engagement ring?"

He fished the ring out of his pocket, secured in a plastic evidence bag, and held it up for me. The plastic couldn't obscure the quality of the diamond in the middle of the setting. It was huge, wreathed by tiny sapphires winking under the lights of the chandeliers.

"The victim had a different diamond on her ring finger, no wedding ring. At an event like this, any woman here could have been wearing a ring like this, so I need to determine if it belonged to Rebecca Yardley or someone else."

I almost corrected him. Any of us who worked for the resort could certainly never afford a ring like that, but I let it go. I knew what he meant, and there was no need to bring it up.

"I'll let you get back to work. Do you know when we might leave? I know you have an investigation to conduct, but we were all up early preparing for the ski team's arrival."

I didn't mention the real reason I wanted to leave was to go talk to the cats. What he didn't need to know wouldn't hurt him.

He smoothed back his hair and looked around the room.

"My officers will have talked to almost everyone now. I'll check with them and see where I need to follow up. I think the staff should be free to leave within the hour. I don't think any of you are guilty."

I met his sky-blue eyes and tried to smile, but missed the mark. I'd forgiven him for springing my background check on me before, but I still felt uncertain around him. I looked away, towards Charlie and Danny, who were watching us with interest.

"Thanks. I'd better go. I hope you discover who killed Rebecca. She didn't deserve to die."

"What? No offers to help solve this case? After last time, I thought I'd have to tear you away."

His boyish grin melted my heart. Just a little. But I forced myself to take a step back, when all I wanted to do was take him up on his offer. His smile faded as I tried to come up with an answer. I failed and shrugged instead.

"I'll let you go," he said, straightening his back. "Be careful, Eden. Until we find out who killed Rebecca Yardley, you might be in danger."

"Me? I have nothing in common with a wealthy, talented athlete. I don't think I'm at risk."

"You both have brown hair, you're around the same age, and you're both incredibly beautiful women. Just... be careful, okay?"

I nodded, tongue tied into a knot. Had he just said I was beautiful? Ethan's cheeks flushed again, and he turned abruptly, walking towards the Yardleys. I stood for a second before rejoining my friends. Denise was waiting with Charlie, Danny, and Wendy as I walked up. She leaned closer.

"Did he say who did it?"

"No, he's still investigating. I think it's someone in this room, though."

I held my tongue about the ring Ethan discovered in the snow. My mind had latched onto that clue and it didn't want to let go. Rebecca was wearing a ring when she was found, so who did it belong to? I looked around the ski team with more interest, focusing my attention on potential suspects. Was Charlie right? Had someone on the team, or an alternate, killed Rebecca? Would they have been wearing a priceless ring?

I shook my head and focused on Charlie, who was staring at me oddly.

"What?"

"I just asked if you knew when we could go and you stared off into space. Are you okay?"

"Sorry, just thinking. Ethan said it would be about an hour."

She leaned down to massage one of her feet with a groan.

"I wish we'd left some of those chairs in here. I'd kill for somewhere to sit right now. I mean, I'd really like to sit down."

Charlie visibly blanched at her word choice as Danny shrugged out of his coat and laid it on the floor next to the wall.

"Here you go. You can sit on that."

Charlie took him up on the offer immediately. She scooted to the side and patted it.

"There's room for you, Eden. Thanks, Danny. That was very thoughtful."

"That'll be five bucks," Danny said, winking at us.

I groaned as he chuckled and sat down, leaning back against the wall. This day had been one of the longest I could remember and it didn't look like it was going to get any shorter. I plotted on how I'd approach the cats as I struggled to stay awake. Charlie leaned into me and within a few minutes, she was snoring softly. I didn't miss the gentle look Danny gave her as he plopped down on her other side and eased her head onto his shoulder.

Chapter Five

T he hour Ethan thought it would take stretched into three, and by the time we could leave the ballroom, any thoughts of trekking through the snow to find the clowder were long gone. The ski team shuffled in front of us as the group made its way towards the lobby. The mood was strained as everyone eyed everyone else with suspicion.

I craned my head around, hoping to spot Ethan. Had he found the killer? There'd been no sign of him arresting anyone, but in all fairness, I'd finally succumbed to sleep halfway through the wait. My eyes felt scratchy as I searched for my coat. Charlie leaned against the front desk, ponytail askew, yawning widely.

"Charlie, you're off for tonight," Mr. Marsburg said, his face grim. "Wendy, you can come in two hours late."

"Mr. Marsburg, that's highly irregular," Penny said as she came up behind him, her posture impeccable as always, despite the late hour. "We must have someone at the desk."

"Miss Langston," Mr. Marsburg said, his shoulders slumped. "I think we'll be fine for a few hours. The only guests are the ski team and if they need something, I'll see to it myself. Your team is dismissed for the night shift as well. We all need sleep. I will be in my office if anyone needs anything."

Penny's lips drew into a tight seam as she watched our boss walk away. Marsburg's shoulders were still slumped, and he walked like a broken man. I slid my arms into the sleeves of my coat, heart aching for him. Even though his engagement to Rebecca ended, his grief was palpable.

"This is highly irregular," Penny said, repeating herself.

"Yes, you are," Charlie said, her temper flaring as bright as she jammed her arms into her coat. "For God's sake, Penny, a woman was killed. Someone he was very close to at one time. Have a little respect."

"I will not be lectured on respect by an upstart girl with oddly colored hair," Penny said, raking Charlie with a look.

I rolled my eyes and drew Charlie towards the door, away from Penny's venom. Danny brought up the rear, swathed in an enormous scarf. We were silent as we made our way to the cabins. I heard someone running behind us and turned to see Wendy trying to catch up.

"Can you believe her?" Wendy said, huffing and puffing. "Why does she always have to be so mean?"

The last thing I wanted was for everyone to get fired up in their mutual dislike of the head of housekeeping. That could keep until tomorrow. I stopped walking and raised a hand.

"It's late, guys, and emotions are running high. Maybe that's just how she deals with uncertainty."

"If by that you mean she doubles down on her typically nasty attitude, you're probably right. Still, she gets under my skin," Charlie said, grumbling. "I think you'd be the last person to defend her."

I shook my head and started walking again.

"Wendy, here's your cabin. Get some rest. If you need any help in the morning, just let me know."

We said our half-hearted goodbyes and continued on down the row until it was just Charlie and me. I stopped at the door of her cabin and leaned against the wood.

"Charlie, if you're going to be up for a few minutes, I can change and bring your dress back."

She yawned, waving me off with a hand.

"Nah. Honestly, I want you to keep it. It looks much better on you than it ever did on me. Besides, did you see the way Ethan looked at you in that dress? It would be a crime to give it back to me," she said before wincing. "Oh God, that was a terrible thing for me to say after what happened. I'm a horrible person."

Her face screwed up, and I reached over to wrap her in a hug.

"Charlie, you've been up for almost twenty-four hours and I don't count napping on the floor, propped up on Danny as sleep. You're a wonderful person. Go get some rest."

She nodded and squeezed me back before opening her door.

"See you tomorrow. My schedule is going to be all thrown off after this. I'm so used to the night shift."

"You'll bounce back. See you later."

She waved and closed the door, and I walked the short distance to my cabin, shivering against the cold. I wasn't used to wearing skirts, let alone in winter, and by the time I walked inside, my skin felt raw. I flipped on the light and saw Jasper on the bed, blinking irritably.

"I'm so sorry, Jasper. That was rude of me. Are your eyes okay?"

He huffed and stood, stretching so hard I could see the bed shake under his paws.

"I'm fine. You were gone for a long time. Did you have fun?"

I stripped off my coat and shook my head as I got everything hung up.

"Not exactly. A woman on the ski team died tonight. We've been closed up in the ballroom while the police did their interviews."

His golden eyes gleamed as he hopped down and stretched again.

"Murder?"

"It looks like it," I said, kicking off my shoes and shuffling over to the kitchenette. "Can I get you some food? Oh darn it, I didn't bring you back anything from the buffet. I'm sorry. It was such a mess."

He followed me and sat, wrapping his tail around his feet.

"I'm not hungry. I'm sure you'll be able to get some leftovers later. What happened?"

I checked the food in his bowls, refreshed his water, and stared into my fridge, trying to decide if I wanted to eat anything before falling into bed. Nothing appealed to me, and I closed the door, scratching my scalp as I walked towards my closet.

"Rebecca Yardley was the one who died. She was found outside, on the patio behind the ballroom."

"That's the one that faces the woods, right? I remember seeing the lights on late at night sometimes."

"That's right. The thing is, my boss was outside with her before she was found. Annie, Trevor's wife, mentioned it to him when we ran into Marsburg near the buffet. He seemed uncomfortable that she'd noticed."

"You don't think he did it?"

I shook my head and tried to shimmy out of the dress without tearing it.

"No. He's such a good man, Jasper. I don't think he'd be capable of killing anyone. But I also heard that he was engaged to Rebecca last year, and it didn't work out. Apparently, she had a new fiance, but they hadn't announced it yet."

I pulled on my snuggliest fleece top and pajama bottoms before padding into the bathroom and staring into the mirror. I hated to undo the braids that Charlie took so much time with, but there was no way I'd be able to sleep with them. I set to work while Jasper joined me.

"Do you think he was jealous and snapped? Lost his head? How was she killed?"

"Ethan said she was strangled, but he wants to wait for the coroner just to make sure."

"Ethan? I should've known when you said the police were here. Valewood is a small town. So, it was a crime of passion. That follows the whole jealousy angle nicely, Eden."

That was the problem, but I didn't want to believe it. I finished undoing the last tiny braid and gently ran a brush through the curls that hadn't quite fallen out yet. If I didn't re-braid my hair before I went to bed, it would be a snarled mess in the morning. I sighed and set to work, tossing my hair over my shoulder so I could reach it easier.

"Ethan also found a ring outside in the snow. He showed it to me, Jasper. It looked like an engagement ring, but Rebecca was already wearing one."

I met Jasper's eyes in the mirror as he shifted behind me. The more I talked, the worse it looked for my boss. What if that had been the ring he'd given her? It certainly looked like something he could afford. I focused back on my braid, finishing the end and tying it off.

"Maybe there's another explanation," Jasper said. "Was anyone else seen outside with her?"

I walked towards the bed and turned back the cover, snuggling into its depths. Jasper hopped up next to me as I propped myself up on pillows. He stretched out, just barely touching my leg, and looked at me, his eyes bright.

"Not that I heard. Trevor asked Josh to pull the security footage. I'm sure Ethan will have asked for that. But he didn't make an arrest, so honestly, I don't know."

"Maybe Trevor will let you see the footage. He did last time."

I nodded and picked at the comforter, questions swirling in my head. If Mr. Marsburg was the killer, what did that mean for everyone who worked here? Would we all lose our jobs? Many of us lived on site, which would mean we'd also lose our homes. What would happen to Jasper and the clowder cats? Worry gnawed at my stomach.

"Maybe. I just don't feel like he could do that. Maybe my judgment is clouded, though. We stand to lose a lot if he's the one."

Jasper patted me with a paw, his golden eyes full of sympathy.

"Tomorrow, you could call Hannah. She might have some advice for you. She's certainly dealt with a lot of strange cases."

I perked up, heart soaring. He was absolutely right. Hannah Murphy was the queen of investigative reporters. If anyone could figure out who killed Rebecca, it was Hannah.

"Great idea, Jasper. I wish I could call her now, but it's late. I'll do that first thing before I go to work."

He kneaded the comforter as I slid down and moved the extra pillows to the side. I wasn't sure I was going to sleep, but having something concrete to do when I woke up might help.

"You'll figure it out, Eden. I believe in you."

He yawned, showing the back of his little pink throat, and settled down, his purr raspy but soothing. I thought about the cat I'd seen. That was something else I could do in the morning. It wouldn't hurt to check on the clowder and make sure they had enough to eat, since Luke had fed them early. Maybe Jasper would want to go with me.

I flipped off the light and snuggled down, smiling as Jasper scooted a little closer to my leg. I stroked his head for a few minutes before my eyes grew heavy with sleep. There was nothing like a warm, purring cat to put your mind at ease. I closed my eyes and surrendered to sleep.

Chapter Six

The strident ring of my phone yanked me upwards, heart racing, in the pitch darkness of my room. I sat there, staring at it, until Jasper hissed, snapping me completely into reality. I fumbled with the screen until I finally hit the accept button.

"Eden! You've got to come to the front desk. Hurry!"

Charlie ended the call before I could ask what was wrong, but the panic in her voice was more than enough to have me struggling to my feet, still wrapped up in my sheet. I kicked it away and put the phone down.

"What on earth?" Jasper asked, his eyes gleaming in the low light of the room.

"I don't know. That was Charlie. Something's going on at the front desk. Why isn't she in her cabin? What time is it?"

I flipped on the light switch, wincing in the bright glare, and hurried to my closet, throwing on a hoodie and a pair of jeans, hopping as I shoved my feet through the fabric. Jasper hopped down from the bed and headed for the kitchenette, mumbling something about humans always being chaos.

Cramming a stocking hat over my head, I didn't even bother with socks, stuffing my feet into my cozy winter boots. I snagged my

winter coat and opened the door, dashing out before I realized I'd
forgotten my phone. I ran back in, grabbed it, tripped over a cat toy,
and scrambled back outside.

"I'll be back, Jasper."

More snow had fallen during the short time I'd been asleep, and
I slipped as I raced for the main building of the resort. The lobby
lights were dim, but I could see Charlie through the glass doors as I
careened through them. Her pale face whipped towards mine.

"Charlie! Are you okay?"

She nodded before putting her finger to her lips and pointed to
her ear, leaning close to whisper.

"Listen."

I stood there, panting, willing my heart to beat at a normal
rhythm, and listened so hard I'd swear my ears creaked. Nothing.

"What?"

"Shh. He went back there about ten minutes ago. I heard raised
voices, so I called you. Something's going on."

"Who went back there? Charlie, what is happening? Why are
you here?"

Lack of sleep made it difficult to tamp down the irritation rising
in my chest from being ripped from my cozy bed.

She led me behind the desk, never taking her eyes off the
hallway that led to the resort offices. I could just about make out the
sound of two men talking.

"I fell asleep right away, but I woke up about two hours ago. I
was bored stiff and wide awake, so I figured I may as well get paid
for it. I came in and Mr. Marsburg went back to his office. Everything was quiet until Ethan got here."

My tired mind tried to stack all the facts together, but the blocks
went tumbling down when she mentioned Ethan's name.

"He's here? Why?"

The sound of a door opening silenced her answer, and we stood
straight as our boss walked down the hall, followed by Ethan. Marsburg's face was taut with frustration as he came to a stop in front
of us.

"Miss Brooks, there's been a misunderstanding and I need to go down to the police station. I shouldn't be long, but can you make sure everything runs smoothly in my absence?"

His overly formal tone was my first clue that this was more than just a misunderstanding. The look on Ethan's face decided it.

"Mr. Marsburg, we need to go," he said, prodding my boss towards the exit.

Anger flashed through Marsburg's eyes, but he nodded stiffly and turned back to face me.

"Please let the senior staff know I will be indisposed. I would appreciate it. I'm confident this will all be settled shortly."

I glanced at Ethan's impassive face. His eyes were hard as ice. A chill worked its way down my spine. James Marsburg was in deep trouble. I focused back on my boss and nodded.

"Of course. We'll make sure everything is handled and goes smoothly. Please let us know if you need anything."

Ethan prodded Marsburg again, and they headed towards the doors. Charlie and I were silent as they slid shut with a whoosh. Our boss raised his shoulders against the cold and followed Ethan to the parking lot. They turned the corner, out of our line of sight.

"He did it, didn't he?" Charlie asked, her eyes filling with tears. "Our boss killed Rebecca Yardley."

Even though those same suspicions were rampaging through my heart, I shook my head. Deep down, I just didn't think it was possible.

"Maybe he's just taking him in for questioning. There might have been something that was unclear, and Ethan just needed to confirm a few things."

The excuse sounded lame even as I spoke, and Charlie gave me a look, shaking her head.

"You know as well as I do if that were true, he'd just ask those questions here and then leave. Our boss just got arrested. The only reason he wasn't handcuffed is because Ethan knows him and was trying to let him cling to a shred of dignity."

I tore off my stocking hat and rumpled it in my hands as I started pacing. She was right, and I knew it. Why hadn't Marsburg just admitted that was what was going on? He had to know we'd figure it out.

"I don't think he did it, Charlie. I just don't. He's always been so kind, so caring. He's not a killer. You've known him longer than I. What do you think?"

Charlie bit her lip and fiddled with the end of her ponytail, a miserable look on her face.

"I wasn't here when he was engaged to Rebecca, but from what Wendy said, he was gutted when it ended. Love can make people do strange things. She wanted to focus on her career, but then a year later, she turned around and was engaged to someone else. I mean, yeah, Marsburg's a great boss, but he's human. I know if someone I'd been engaged to showed up at my hotel about to announce their new engagement, I'd be pretty upset."

"But would you be upset enough to kill them? To kill them on your hotel property, after everyone saw you talking to them outside? No. He'd have a neon sign hanging over his head proclaiming his guilt. I'm not buying it."

Charlie leaned back against the desk and crossed her arms over her chest.

"Okay, so who killed her?"

I stopped pacing and shoved my hat in my coat pocket.

"I don't know, but we're going to find out. We need evidence, hard evidence, that Marsburg's innocent," I said, shrugging out of my coat. "Trevor mentioned security footage. We can start there. Is Josh still on duty?"

Charlie nodded, her face lighting with hope.

"I think so. Let's go back and see him. He should be in his office."

I headed down the hall but skidded to a stop when I saw Marsburg's office. The light was still on and its usual ordered state was drastically changed. Papers were everywhere. I walked in, Charlie at my heels, and looked around.

"Should we be in here?" Charlie asked, craning her head around.

"Probably not, but we need to switch the light off," I said, scanning the room. "Why is everything so messy? I've never seen his desk like this."

My fingers skimmed the papers haphazardly stacked, itching to read through them.

"Eden, what's this?" Charlie asked, moving to the credenza behind the desk.

I turned to see what she was pointing at and saw a picture frame, face down. I'd met with my boss in his office a few times, but I'd never paid attention to the pictures. I picked up the frame and sighed. It was a picture of Rebecca and Marsburg, smiling happily.

"He was grieving and turned it over, not wanting to see the woman he once loved, right?" I asked, hoping it was true.

"Maybe. Or..."

She didn't need to finish. I studied the picture harder, looking for Rebecca's left hand. My stomach sank as I recognized the ring on her finger. I tapped the glass and held it towards Charlie.

"That's the ring Ethan found in the snow. I'd know it anywhere."

Charlie's face fell as she took the frame from my numb fingers.

"It's a beautiful ring. Eden, this looks bad. Terrible."

"I know, but we can't assume. Until we ask Marsburg ourselves, there's no way to know what he was thinking when he turned this over."

She bit her lip again and opened her mouth, but shut it as a bell sounded from the lobby.

"Oh shoot, I gotta go. Someone's up front."

She handed me the frame and hustled out of the office. I looked at it for a few more seconds before I put it back on the credenza, just like we'd found it. My steps were slow as I turned around to leave, flipping off the light switch and shutting the door.

I heard Charlie and another woman talking in the lobby and headed in their direction, our visit to Josh forgotten. When I got to the desk, I found Charlie talking with the youngest member of the ski team. I smiled as I joined them.

"Alicia, right?"

She nodded, but didn't smile. Her sunburned face was dusted lightly with freckles.

"I'm going to show her where the sauna is. Do you want to tag along, Eden?" Charlie asked, tossing me a meaningful look.

"Sure."

"You don't have to go to all this trouble," Alicia said, playing with the tail end of her strawberry blonde braid. "Just point me in the right direction. I can find it."

"It's no bother," Charlie said, brightly. "I'm so sorry about what happened last night. How is the team holding up?"

Alicia snorted before coloring and holding her hand to her mouth as I walked beside her.

"Sorry, that was rude. I still can't believe Rebecca's gone. I keep expecting it to all be a dream and I'll see her coming down the steps. She's the one who recommended I use the sauna after I hurt my knee a few months ago. I've done it religiously, every morning, ever since. I didn't want to go this morning, but I couldn't sleep, and here I am. It just felt wrong not to do it, but it feels wrong to do it at the same time. Does that make any sense?"

She looked at me, as though mystified she shared so much, and I nodded in understanding.

"Routine can be a very helpful way of working through grief. I'm the same way. I find it easier to focus on my usual steps. Have you been with the team for long?"

I glanced at her face as we walked. She was young, much younger than the other members of the team.

"About eight months. One of the other girls left after getting pregnant and a spot opened up. I've been training since I was five, but I never thought I'd get the opportunity. Sometimes I still can't believe it."

"Wow, since you were five?" Charlie asked. "That's dedication. What's your event?"

"Super G. I'm still training in Slalom, but G is where I'm most comfortable."

The terms flew right over my head, and I made a mental note to research them later.

"What did Rebecca do?"

Alicia's footsteps slowed, and she hunched her shoulders, folding into herself.

"Slalom. She was the best," she said, her voice hitching. "I suppose Sassy's going to take her place, unless Kendra can step up. I'm not good enough to take her spot. I guess they'll have to see which one is better."

"Kendra?"

"She's an alternate for the team. She was delayed, but she got in last night, right before the banquet."

I looked behind Alicia and met Charlie's eyes. Maybe we'd just found our first suspect.

"Is the team pretty competitive, or do you each have your own specialized area?"

Alicia furrowed her brow and tilted her head back and forth.

"I mean, each member has their strengths, as well as other events we're trying to dominate. It just depends. Slalom is one the hardest, it's just so technical. I'm fast, so that's why I prefer Super G. You've got to be fantastic to compete at that level."

"What's Sassy's other event?" Charlie asked. "Here's the gym room. You can swipe your card to get in."

Alicia put her card through the reader and Charlie held open the door for her.

"She does downhill, and she'd alternate with Becca on the combined. Unless Kendra can put together some good runs, I suppose Sassy will take Becca's spot."

I added another suspect to the list and looked at Charlie again. She nodded briefly before pointing out the sauna.

"Here you go. It's an infrared one. I hope that's okay. We haven't turned on it for the day yet, so it will take a little while to come to temp."

"That's okay. All of our training today was canceled, so I have time. I'll probably work out while it heats. Thanks for showing me everything. That was nice of you."

Charlie and I smiled.

"If you need anything, just use the phone on that wall," Charlie said, pointing towards the hotel phone. "There should be plenty of towels."

Alicia's smile was tinged with sadness as she walked over to the leg press machine. We turned to leave her to it, and I followed Charlie as she led the way back to the front desk.

"Did you hear that about Kendra? Is she staying here? I'd like to talk to her. She was here at the banquet, but I don't know what she looked like."

"Let's check," Charlie said, picking up speed. "It still doesn't explain the ring, though."

My steps faltered. She was right. It didn't explain the ring. But it gave us at least one more person who had a motive to see Rebecca Yardley dead. I waved off my doubts and kept moving.

Chapter Seven

I left Charlie at the front desk to check on Kendra's status and went back to my cabin. I needed to call Hannah, and I still wanted to check with the cats in the clowder to see if they'd seen anything. Jasper was waiting for me, bright of eye and bushy of tail.

"You were gone forever," he said, coming forward to give me a quick bump on the leg. "What's going on?"

"I think Marsburg was taken in for Rebecca's murder," I said, walking over to the kitchenette to get him his breakfast.

I busied myself scooping food out of a can. Jasper hopped onto the counter, sniffed the food briefly before he looked at me, quirking his whiskers.

"Think? That's a strange way of putting it."

"Well, Ethan didn't come right out and say it, but it was definitely implied. Marsburg seems to think it's all a misunderstanding, but..."

"You're not sure. Humans."

"I'm almost certain he didn't kill her. But I found a picture of Rebecca in his office wearing the ring Ethan found last night."

The look on Jasper's face spoke volumes. I slid the bowl over to him and gave him a quick pet before rinsing out the can in the sink.

As I puttered around the small space, I told Jasper about running into Alicia and what she'd said about Sassy and Kendra.

"Hmmm," he said, before swiping his bowl clean of the remaining gravy. "Rivalry is always a powerful motive for murder. Even among cats, it's not unheard of for a leader to be challenged. Of course, we don't go around murdering each other, not like humans do. Cats are much more straightforward."

I picked up his bowl and washed it, setting aside to dry in the dish rack, while Jasper washed up.

"Were you ever challenged?"

His paw stilled and his golden eyes met mine.

"Once. When Oscar first arrived, he had big ambitions about leading the clowder. It was a fierce fight, but experience trumped brute strength."

Oscar. I thought about the black cat with striking blue eyes from the clowder. Jasper was worried that Fig would have issues with the cat, but so far, she'd managed him nicely. If it came to a battle, my money would be on Fig. She wasn't a cat to be messed with. I looked out my window towards the woods before turning to Jasper.

"Would you like to come with me to visit them? I want to ask if anyone saw anything last night, and I can't wait until my usual time tonight."

Jasper stretched, fluffing out his fur.

"Of course. I want to check on Luna. Her litter is due soon. I'm sure Fig's got it all under control, but I'd like to see for myself."

I unzipped my coat, picked him up, and tucked him to my chest. His familiar rusty purr started deep in his chest. As we walked outside, I shivered and checked to make sure he was secure and warm.

"Isn't it the wrong time of year for kittens?" I asked.

Jasper snorted, curling close to my warmth.

"Tell that to Luna and Oscar. They know better. The clowder will ensure the kits are safe and warm, but it's more work for everyone."

I hesitated, wanting to bring up my plans to fix the clowder cats, but uncertain how best to broach the subject. Now was as

good a time as any. I was just about to start when I heard
someone call my name. I turned and spotted Luke waving madly
in front of the dining hall. I waved back and hustled over there,
picking my way through the piles of snow that drifted during the
night.

"Good morning, Eden. Are you heading to the clowder by any
chance?"

Jasper poked his head out of my coat and Luke smiled, his hazel
eyes lighting. He was wearing a short-sleeve shirt under his apron
and he had to be freezing.

"We are. What's up?"

"Hello, Mr. Jasper," Luke said, nodding at the cat. "I've got
some eggs that were scrambled by mistake and I thought the cats
might like them. I was going to put them aside, but they'd be much
better warm. I spotted you through the window and thought I'd
check."

"Sure, I'll be happy to take them to the cats. Do cats like eggs?"

Luke shrugged before dashing back inside. I directed my question to Jasper.

"I can't say that I've ever eaten eggs before. I won't know unless
I try. But these are for the clowder, not me."

Luke reappeared, carrying a plastic grocery bag filled with
containers.

"I threw in some bacon that got a little burnt. The kitchen has
been in chaos ever since we heard about Mr. Marsburg."

He trailed off, a miserable expression on his face. I nodded,
catching on quickly. The news must have spread like wildfire if the
kitchen already knew about it.

"I don't think he did it, Luke. We've just got to hope justice will
be done."

A shout came from the kitchens and Luke started, his face
flushing.

"I've got to go. See you later, Eden."

He dashed back inside, gangly limbs flailing, and I returned to
my trek to the woods. Steam leaked out of the bag as I walked, and
Jasper sniffed appreciatively.

"The bacon smells good, at least. I'm still not sure about the eggs."

I kept walking, huddled against the cold, worrying about the cats. Even with their winter coats, they had to be freezing. My heart ached imagining tiny kittens being brought into the world in the dead of winter.

We hadn't made it very far into the woods when Jasper started squirming in my coat. I knew the drill. He didn't mind me carrying him, but he preferred to stand on his own four feet around the clowder. I stopped and unzipped my coat, allowing him to jump free. Somehow, he landed on a stump, bypassing the drifted snow.

"That was an incredible jump," I said, smothering a grin as he preened. "Where do you think they are this morning?"

I typically only came at night, and I wasn't sure what the clowder did during the day. There was so much to learn about these amazing cats. Luckily, we didn't have to wait long. I saw Fig carefully picking her way around the snow.

"Not that I'm not happy to see you, Jasper, but what are you doing out here?"

Jasper straightened on the stump, whiskers bristling.

"We have a question and we brought food."

Fig sniffed the air, her startling yellow eyes flaring.

"I smell bacon and something else."

"Eggs," I said, holding up the bag. "Luke wasn't sure if you'd like them, but I'm a big fan of them."

Her lip curled delicately as I tried to figure out how best to portion out the containers Luke sent. I spotted the area where we usually fed them and walked over to clear the snow as Jasper and Fig bent their heads together. She turned and sent up a yowl that echoed in the thin morning air. One by one, cats began appearing.

Once I had the snow cleared off the platter as best I could, I began unpacking the food, laying it out as carefully as I could. A white cat with rounded sides approached first, her steps tentative.

"Luna?" I asked, remaining crouched down, so I didn't startle her.

Her pretty eyes went wide, and she nodded, approaching cautiously.

"What are those things?"

"Eggs. I think they'd probably be good for the kits if you'd like to try them. Eggs are full of protein."

She touched her tiny pink tongue to the eggs and took a tentative nibble. Her shocked expression lasted about a second before she began wolfing them down.

"Hey, let me try some," Ollie, the rotund tuxedo cat, said as he stomped forward. "Is that bacon?"

"Ollie, wait your turn," Fig snapped. "You know the rules."

He halted and waited as the younger cats came forward to taste the eggs. I laughed softly in delight at their varied expressions as they each took a small mouthful. By the time everyone had sampled the eggs, I put it at about a fifty-fifty ratio of egg lovers to those who couldn't stand them. The bacon, however, was a definite hit.

I waited until Fig was done with her share. The leader of the clowder always ate last, after everyone else had their fill. I looked at her skinny sides in concern. They needed more food. I'd have to ask Luke if we could spare more leftovers.

Even though my feet were numb from the cold, I waited until Fig had finished washing up. Pressuring her never ended well. She was a stickler, but I knew that was a good thing. She ran the clowder with an iron paw, and even though she was tough, she was fair. She noticed me watching her and lowered her paw, huffing out a sight.

"Out with it. Jasper said you had a question."

Her tone couldn't fool me. She'd saved my life when Emma attacked, and I knew the brown cat was nicer than she let on.

"Was anyone from the clowder near the main lodge last night? I saw a cat but I couldn't tell who it was. I was hoping they saw something. A terrible thing happened last night and they might be the only witness."

She tilted her head to the side, studying my face.

"Another murder? I swear humans are the most brutal creatures. It wasn't me, but I'll ask."

She turned to the clowder, who was spread out in little groups. They immediately came to attention as she spoke.

"Was anyone near the big wooden building last night? I know I had no patrols over in that direction, but I'll let it slide since apparently, the human needs help again."

My lips quirked at her tone. Apparently, I was a human that could be tolerated, only with great forbearance.

The cats shook their heads, murmuring quietly. Finally, a soft voice caught my ear. A delicate cat with a beautiful tortoiseshell coat stepped forward.

"I was in the woods, but I saw that cat again last night. He was coming from that direction."

I turned, a question on my lips, as Fig shook her head, fluffing out her coat.

"He's not one of us. Sometimes we get stragglers who want to join the clowder. Depending on their attitude, we take them in, especially in the winter. Everyone needs shelter and if they can hunt, they're always welcome. This cat, however, has not approached us. He seems content to exist on the outskirts. I haven't sought him out."

She looked at Jasper, who gave her an approving nod before speaking.

"Not everyone is built for clowder life. I was once that way, preferring to be alone. As long as they don't take too much game, it's never been a big deal. There's plenty for all."

My shoulders slumped, but I turned to the tortoiseshell cat.

"Thank you. I appreciate it. What's your name?"

"I'm Willow," she said, shyly ducking her head. "If I see him again, I will try to ask him for you. Thank you for the eggs. They were delicious."

She darted a look at Fig before melting back into the shadows of the trees. The clowder's leader turned to me and heaved another sigh.

"I suppose if I see him, I'll talk to him, too. There's no guarantee he'll meddle in the lives of humans. Some cats prefer not to."

Her expression said she was one of those cats, but I knew underneath that surly exterior beat a heart that was true and brave. If she could help me, she would. She rubbed her head on Jasper's side and they exchanged a few quiet words before she gave a sharp cry and led the cats back into the trees.

Ollie was the only one who stayed, sniffing the platter as if he hoped he could conjure more eggs. I let out a short laugh at his forlorn expression.

"I'll let Luke know you like eggs, Ollie. Maybe we can bring more sometime."

He brightened, green eyes gleaming, and swiped his tongue around his muzzle.

"Much appreciated, ma'am. I'll see if I can find that cat for you."

He sauntered off into the trees, tail held high. I heard a sigh from the stump and turned to see Jasper watching the remaining cats as they disappeared into the trees. Did he miss this life? A twinge went through my heart. I'd grown so close to him and couldn't imagine sending him back here to live.

"Ready to go?" I asked, my voice soft.

His eyes met mine, and he nodded as I refilled the plastic bag with the containers to return to Luke.

"Let's go. Fig's doing a great job with them. Everyone looks good."

That was all he said on our walk back to the cabin, but I could tell his mind was going a hundred miles an hour. I opened the door and stepped inside, grateful for the warmth of the heater making the cabin so cozy. I put Jasper on the bed and set to work rinsing the containers, desperate for something to do, and not wanting to leave just yet. Jasper stared at the door from his place on the bed before turning his golden eyes in my direction.

"It would be a shame to deprive Fig of her role, wouldn't it? She's worked hard, and the clowder is thriving. I don't think they need me anymore."

His face was inscrutable, but his words were heavy. As much as I wanted him to stay with me, I knew what the clowder meant to him.

I'd done my best to convince him to stay, and he'd extended his deadline several times.

"Jasper, I..."

He shot me a look and his whiskers curled up. He turned in a circle a few times before settling down into the comforter.

"I think I'll stay here, at least for now," he said, his voice muffled as he wrapped his tail around his face. "I don't know what you'd do without me. And it's a good thing to be needed."

My heart almost burst as joy poured through it. I quietly walked over to him and carefully kissed him on his little forehead. Tears poured down my cheeks, landing on his soft fur.

"Thank you, Jasper."

His rusty purr filled the room, and I couldn't believe it as he swiped his rough tongue over my cheek. He was staying!

Chapter Eight

B reakfast was an unusually somber affair. Instead of the usual chatter and bickering, the only sound was forks clanking on plates. Danny sullenly pushed his hash browns around his plate, mixing them with his scrambled eggs.

"I don't know how it got out so quickly," Charlie said, her voice hushed. "I didn't say a thing."

"Carl saw Marsburg get into Ethan's car, and he told Iris in the kitchen, and here we are. Soon to be tossed out on the street. Well, it was a nice gig while it lasted."

He sighed and then forked the rest of his breakfast into his mouth. Charlie's fork clattered to the table as she shook her head.

"No, we're not going quietly into that dark night," she said, hair flying. "We've already got other suspects lined up. Don't be so quick to clap our boss behind bars. It's possible he didn't do it. Like, super possible."

She lacked the enthusiasm to make her words believable, but I appreciated the effort.

"Nice Dylan Thomas reference, Charlie. I'm following up on a few leads as well. And we still need to talk to Josh. It's possible there's video evidence that will clear Marsburg and all this worry is for nothing."

A heavy sigh behind me prompted me to turn my head, and I saw Trevor behind us. His plate was heaped with food, as per usual, but as he sat heavily in the chair next to me, he stared at it instead of digging in.

"I saw the video stream last night. It shows Marsburg talking with her, but then they moved out of the line of sight of the camera. He came back into view when he walked back inside, but Rebecca never did. It doesn't look good, guys."

My mind raced with possibilities and I grabbed one in a mental death grip.

"Okay, so they went outside to talk. We don't know what they were discussing, but likely it had something to do with their prior engagement. What if our boss said what he had to say, left, and then someone else came around on the other side, completely out of view of the camera and strangled Rebecca? Are there any other feeds that could back up that theory?"

I turned to Trevor, full of excitement, and watched as he slowly chewed a piece of bacon. He nodded slowly.

"I mean, it's possible. Every exit door has a camera. We focused on the one in the ballroom, but not the others. We might have been grasping at straws, but I can't believe Marsburg would hurt a fly. Maybe you're right, Eden. I'll go check the other feeds."

He scraped his chair back and hustled out of the dining hall, leaving his plate behind. Danny eyed the remaining bacon and snagged a piece, waving it in the air as he munched on it.

"Well, that's positive. Great thinking, Eden."

Charlie didn't react as he waved the bacon in front of her face. She turned to me and lowered her voice.

"She was strangled?"

"I think so. That's what Ethan said last night. But he wanted to hear from the coroner before he released it. I shouldn't have said anything."

"Whoever did it would have to be strong, right? I mean, Rebecca was tall. I'm about five-five, and she towered over me. She was a professional athlete, she would've fought back. You saw Alicia this morning. She's not that big, but she's ripped. They train constantly."

I slowly put my fork down, appetite gone. Charlie was right. I drummed my fingers on the table as I thought.

"So, the killer would need to be at least as tall as Rebecca, or close to her size, and strong enough to overpower her. Does that rule out Sassy and Kendra?"

"Who's Kendra?" Danny asked as he grabbed a roll off Trevor's plate, ignoring the irritated tsking sound from Charlie. "What? He won't eat it and it would be a shame to let it go stale."

Charlie rolled her eyes.

"Okay, bottomless pit. Kendra is the alternate who shows the most promise in the slalom, Rebecca's main discipline. She didn't show up with the team, which is suspicious."

"Is she hot?" Danny asked, winking as he chewed.

"Gross. Both the comment and the pastry flakes you're spewing everywhere," Charlie said, cheeks flushing red.

I stepped in before the bickering got worse. Charlie didn't seem to realize she was being baited by Danny and I would not be the one to bring it up. Not now.

"I haven't met her, but I plan to track her down. Charlie, did you find out which room she's staying in?"

"She's in 322," Charlie said, pushing back from the table in a huff and grabbing her plate. "If you'll excuse me, I'm going to my cabin to catch up on some sleep. I'll see you in a couple of hours, Eden."

I watched her walk to the bussing station, back straight, and turned to see Danny staring at her, a mystified expression stamped on his face.

"What did I say?"

"I think you know exactly what you said and why you said it. Look, Danny, I don't know how you feel about Charlie, but if you like her, you're going about it all wrong."

His cheeks flushed as red as Charlie's, and he looked down at his plate. I noticed he didn't contradict me, so I filed that away for the future, when I wasn't trying to prove our boss was innocent. I grabbed my tray, ready to stand, and nearly bumped into Penny. How long had she been standing there?"

"Gossiping again, are we? Don't you people have anything better to do?"

She looked down her nose, sneered, and walked towards another table, where her staff was grouped. I saw their shoulders tighten from behind as she banged her tray down and pointedly looked at her watch. Thank goodness she wasn't in charge of me. I couldn't imagine having Penny as a manager.

I bussed my tray and walked back to the main building, hands jammed in my pockets. A shout turned me back, and I spotted Danny slipping and sliding on an icy patch as he tried to catch up with me.

"Eden, say nothing. To Charlie, I mean. I know you two are close."

I exhaled a frustrated cloud of steam into the morning air.

"You guys need to work it out between yourselves. I'm not getting involved. But Daniel Cooper, I swear, if you hurt her, I will come for you. Charlie is an amazing woman, and she deserves the best."

He held up his hands and hung his head miserably.

"I wouldn't hurt her. I'm just not sure, you know? We're friends now, and have been for months. I don't wanna mess it up."

Given my track record of relationships, and by that, I meant one that failed spectacularly, I was in no place to offer any advice. All I knew was that Charlie had welcomed me with open arms and was quickly becoming the best friend I'd ever had.

"Take your time, Danny. Be sure. I can tell you have feelings for her, but don't rush it, okay? If something's going to happen, it will happen. Naturally. Just try not to say stupid things, okay?"

I softly punched him in the arm and he grabbed it, mock wounded.

"Ow! Remind me never to cross you. Thanks, Eden. I appreciate it."

He tipped an imaginary hat to me, and I groaned. He was such a character. If it worked out for them, Charlie would never be short of laughs. She might be short of potatoes, though.

He whistled as we walked into the lobby, spotting Wendy behind the desk. Her face was drawn as she stared into space. She'd obviously heard the news. Danny split off, leaving me alone with her.

"Hey, Wendy. Everything okay?"

"I just can't believe it," she said. "It can't be. He's such a nice man."

I went around the desk and gave her a one-armed hug.

"We don't know what happened, Wendy. We can't jump to conclusions. That's the worst thing we could do. You look so nice. Is that a new sweater? I liked the one you wore yesterday, too."

She took a shaky breath and smoothed her fuzzy sweater. It was a beautiful orange color that brought out the green in her hazel eyes.

"It is. I just had my color palette done and I'm trying new colors in my season. Do you really like it?"

I didn't know what color palettes and seasons were, but she was radiant, and I nodded enthusiastically.

"You're beautiful."

"I know it's silly, but I've always had a crush on St. John and I wanted to look my best. I know he wouldn't look twice at a frump like me."

"Hey! You're not a frump. Maybe I should get my seasons done. I never have a clue what looks best."

Her eyes brightened before narrowing as she looked at my face. She grabbed my chin and turned it back and forth.

"Soft summer. You're muted and slightly cool."

I didn't know what to do with that information, but I filed it away in case I ever got the hankering to buy new clothes.

"Thanks, I'll have to look into it. Now, I need to do a little sleuthing. Are you willing to help?"

She nodded, curls bouncing, and looked around the empty lobby.

"You think he's innocent, don't you?"

"I do. And there are a few people I need to talk to. Can you watch the lobby and text me if you see Penny? I don't want her to know what I'm doing."

"Of course," she said, straightening.

I smiled and patted her arm.

"Great. Do you know what room Sassy Jermain is in?"

She cocked an eyebrow but turned to her computer and tapped on it.

"She's in 324. We put the whole ski team on the same floor. Rebecca was in 321, next to her brother."

Maybe I'd luck out and be able to talk to the ski team members individually. One of them had to have information that could clear our boss. At least I hoped so.

"Thanks, Wendy. Talk to you soon."

I walked to the elevator bay and punched the button. The doors immediately slid open, and I darted in. It felt good to be doing something productive. I ended up on the third floor and turned left, towards the wing where the ski team was housed. My steps slowed as I realized I needed a better plan. Was I just going to waltz up to their rooms, knock, and ask if they killed Rebecca?

The door to 322 swung open right as I ended up in front of it and a girl walked out, yawning. Her highlighted brown hair was rumpled, and she looked out of it.

"Kendra?"

"Yeah?" she rasped, blinking at me strangely. "Who are you?"

"I'm Eden Brooks, with the hotel's PR department," I said, thinking on the fly. "I'm just checking on everyone after what happened last night to make sure you're okay and see if you need anything."

Dang, maybe I was better under pressure than I thought. Kendra's face crumpled, and she burst into tears. Okay... maybe I wasn't.

"I can't believe it," she said, wailing so loudly she would surely rouse the entire floor. "Why did this happen to me?"

I blinked, startled at the direction her mind took, and grabbed her arm, hustling her into the room. Either she was messy, or she just hadn't finished putting all of her things away. Clothes were everywhere, and I tripped over a pair of large boots on my way towards the only chair in the room.

"Here, sit. I'm so sorry to upset you. Can I get you anything?"

She collapsed into the chair in a dramatic heap and whimpered.

"Maybe a glass of champagne? It might help settle my nerves."

Her tears had miraculously dried up as she angled her face up, eyes huge. I wasn't sure, but I was betting she wasn't twenty-one.

"I'll see what I can do. In the meantime, let me get you some water and some tissues."

She buried her face in her hands as I bustled around the room, grabbing a glass and a bottle of water out of the mini-fridge. I put the glass on the table next to her and passed her some tissues. She wadded them in her hands and looked at me, eyes dry. I sat on top of the coffee table and waited for her to speak.

"Thanks. It's such a trying time. Why is this happening to me?"

She took a noisy gulp of her water before sobbing into her tissues. What was going on here? I opened my mouth, only to shut it as someone rapped on the door. I hopped to my feet and motioned towards Kendra.

"I'll get it."

I'd no sooner opened the door when Sassy Jermain flounced in, hair flying. It took her a second to realize someone other than Kendra opened the door. She looked between us, face set in a hard expression.

"Who the hell are you?"

"I'm Eden Brooks, with the hotel's PR team. I'm making sure everyone's okay."

They didn't need to know that the team comprised one person, me, and apparently, it didn't matter. Sassy flung herself backward on the bed and let out a groan.

"Ugh, go away. Can't you see we're dealing with our grief? Sassy, did you hear what Chris said? The team is pulling out of the slalom race and we might not even compete at the event now, all in remembrance of Becca."

The way she said Rebecca's name made me want to make sure

the bedding hadn't been burned by the acid dripping from her tongue. A startled shriek from Kendra distracted me.

"What?! You've got to be kidding me!"

I glanced between the two women. Another knock at the door had me wandering towards it in a daze. I opened it, completely unsurprised to see Jude and Troy standing there, faces drawn. They didn't even look at me as they hurried into the room. What was going on here? This was not what I expected.

Chapter Nine

E very available spot to sit in Kendra's room was taken as the ski
team crowded around, and apparently, forgot I existed. That
was just fine with me. I edged towards the door and did my best to
blend into the background, fascinated by the team dynamic.

The blond guy, Jude, sprawled out next to Sassy on the bed,
fiddling with the ends of her hair.

"I know Chris is close to the Yardleys and all, but this is a little
much, don't you think?" he asked, shaking his head. "I mean, we've
all known Becca for most of our lives and we're ready to compete.
It's what she'd want."

"Yeah, man," Troy chimed in as he slouched against the dresser
near Kendra. "The show must go on. She was super stoked for this
event, so like, why can't we do it in her honor or something? She
would have liked that. I mean, I could see Rob not wanting to
compete, but Sam would step up in a heartbeat. You know his times
have been better than Rob's and he's been squawking at Chris to
give him a chance. Hey, speaking of Sam, where's he?"

"Probably in the gym with Alicia," Sassy said, rolling her eyes.
"He's all about her lately. Personally, I don't know what he sees her
in. I mean, have you seen the clothes she wears? Ugh."

My ears perked up, but I bit my tongue before I could ask who Sam was. Right now, I wanted to stay quiet and see what else I could learn.

"True, I totally forgot about Sam. You know, we should all go corner Chris. If we all stand united and say we want to do it in Becca's honor, maybe he'll change his mind."

"I dunno," Kendra said, her tone dull. "You know how close he is to Ash. They've been friends, for like, ever. If Ash is all broken up about losing Becca, he'll influence Chris."

Jude snorted loudly as he flipped Sassy's hair over her face, earning him a shove. She rolled over on the bed to glare at him.

"What's that for?"

"Just playing."

He held up his hands, his handsome face split by a grin as Sassy narrowed her eyes at him and poked him with her finger.

"No, not my hair, although that was rude. I meant the snort."

"Didn't you hear?"

"Hear what?" Troy said, leaning forward.

He wasn't the only one. It was all I could to stay quiet and keep in the background. This ski team was a cesspool of gossip and in-fighting, and I was totally here for it. With every word that came out of their mouths, my belief in Marsburg's innocence grew by leaps and bounds.

"Dude, Rob just caught Ash with that snow bunny in Granby, and you know, he went straight to Becca with the news. He never liked Ash, and word was, she was about to kick him to the curb. She was all about James last night. Ash was all butt-hurt about it. He didn't want to lose his lift ticket, if you know what I mean."

So many terms I didn't understand. I wished Charlie was with me to translate. Sassy threw her head back and laughed.

"Oh God, that is so funny. I always wondered if little miss perfect was going to figure out he was a player. Everyone, and I mean everyone, has had a turn with that guy. But mummy and daddy loved him so it was all good."

She finished her sentence at a sing song, ending with a nasty laugh. Wow, she really did not like Rebecca.

"Geez, Sass. Have a little respect," Troy said, looking at the floor. "I mean, Becca isn't even cold yet. Hey, you over there."

It took me a second to realize he was talking to me.

"God, you're still here? Rude! Why are you eavesdropping?" Sassy said, levering herself off the bed to glare at me.

I stammered for a second, but Troy walked over, a soft smile on his face, and leaned next to me.

"Put away the claws, Sass. What's your name, sweetheart?"

My neck stiffened at his tone. I'd known a man like him before, and it hadn't ended well. I may not know much, but I'd learned the hard way to avoid men dripping with false charm. I put a little distance between us.

"Eden Brooks. I'm the head of PR at the hotel. I came up to see if anyone needed anything, and it seemed rude to leave before I spoke with all of you."

"Oh, how sweet," Troy said, erasing the distance I'd put between us. "You're very thoughtful. Hey, have you heard anything about Rebecca? Rob's with her folks, and we got the run around last night by that cop. What happened?"

I froze, uncertain of how much I should share. Would Ethan mind if I told them their teammate was strangled? I had to say something. I went with it, hoping for the best.

"The early report is that she was strangled," I said, holding up a hand and rushing on when Troy opened his mouth to ask more questions. "But that's still just an assumption. I think the police are waiting on the official coroner's report to release the actual cause of death."

Kendra let out a gasp and put her hand to her chest.

"That poor girl. What a terrible way to go. Do you know if they know who did it?"

She'd arranged her face into a look of concern, but it rang false. Was she asking because she hoped she wasn't a suspect? She was at least as tall as Rebecca. She could've strangled her. Maybe.

"I think they've taken a few people in for questioning," I said, unwilling to throw my boss under the bus. "It's going to take some time to investigate, I'm sure."

"Wow," Jude said. "That's so heavy. I wonder if Ash did it. Did you see him last night? He was all chummy with her parents, but he kept glaring daggers at Becca. Did you hear her dad was going to hire him at the firm?"

"Who knows? It certainly wasn't one of us," Sassy said, before turning to glare at me again. "Is that why you're here? How do we know you work for the hotel? Are you a cop?"

Kendra paled and edged closer to her purse on the table. Interesting.

"She was with the staff at the welcome party, silly," Troy said, leaning even closer as he turned to me. "I noticed you right away. Your hair is dope. Is that extensions or is it all real?"

He reached for my braid. I stepped back and swung it over my shoulder. I'd overstayed my welcome, and I had more than enough information to go on. For now, anyway. At this moment, I didn't want to be in Troy's presence for another millisecond. He gave me the creeps.

"If you'll excuse me, I need to get back to work. If anyone needs anything, please call the front desk. Wendy or Charlie will be happy to assist."

"Oh, can we get some food sent to our rooms? But not like the food last night at the buffet. Like proper food. You know, some steaks or lobster or something? We're in training and we're used to a higher standard."

I blinked at Sassy, appalled at her rudeness. The kitchen staff had worked their tails off for the banquet.

"I'll see what I can do."

I pulled open the heavy door, struggling for an embarrassing second. Troy helped me and smiled.

"See you around, Eden. I like that name."

I suppressed a shudder, but it was a close thing. I refused to turn around as I headed for the elevator, but I could feel his eyes on me. I pressed the down button a few times and nearly jumped for joy as the doors slid open. Once they were shut, I let out a sigh and leaned against the wall.

I popped into the lobby and walked past the front desk. Wendy had the phone to her ear and waved as I went by. I headed for my office, mind spinning. I'd gone from maybe two suspects to an entire room full in just a few minutes with the team. If I didn't get organized, I might miss something important.

I kicked the doorstop out of the way and rummaged through the small supply closet in my office, nearly crowing with delight when I found a whiteboard. I leaned it against the wall and rummaged around until I'd found a dry erase marker. Perfect!

I was deep in thought, scribbling away, when a sharp rap on my door startled me. Charlie's grinning face popped through and she sang out.

"Here's Charlie!"

I cocked my head to the side as she rolled her eyes and walked in, popping away at her gum.

"That won't mean much until we have our movie night. Hey, why didn't you answer my texts? I was worried about you. Whoa, what do we have here?"

"I'm sorry! I've been working on this and didn't even think of my phone. I must have it on silent. What's up?"

"My sleep schedule is all thrown off. I got about an hour long nap and then I was up and bored. You've been busy. What's all this?"

I waved my hand, remembering I needed her help to decipher a few things the ski team said.

"Charlie, what's a snow bunny?"

She cracked her gum loudly before busting out in a laugh, holding onto her sides. I crossed my arms, waiting for her hilarity to taper off.

"Oh my, I didn't expect those words to come out of your mouth. A snow bunny is a rather derogatory term for a woman who doesn't really ski, but hangs out in ski lodges, hoping to snag a rich and or famous boyfriend. Where on earth did you hear that?"

I explained what I'd overheard with the ski team, and Charlie's face brightened as I laid out my new list of suspects. She turned back to the whiteboard and scanned over what I'd written. I'd nearly filled the space. At this rate, I was going to need a second one.

"Wow, you've been busy. So, we've got Kendra, who we knew about it, and potentially Sassy, who sounds like a real treat. You've added Ash, the fiance. Who is Sam, and why is he here?" she asked, pointing at his name.

"Oh, he's the alternate that's been wanting to take Rob's place. It's a longshot, but what if he killed Rebecca, to throw off Rob, and take his spot?"

"Hmmm. I suppose you never know. I mean, that would be pretty diabolical. Why do you have devil horns drawn over the 'o' in Troy's name?"

I colored as I used my finger to smudge those out.

"Sorry. He reminded me of someone I knew."

Charlie sobered, and she pulled me into a one-armed hug. I'd told her about my disastrous relationship with Adam Caldwell. She grabbed the marker and drew the horns back, adding an evil face and stink lines. I couldn't help but giggle as she finished.

"There, that's better. Okay, so we've got a metric ton of suspects. What do we do now?"

I took the marker back and played with it, taking the cap off and on. My goal had been to organize the suspect list, but this was just the start. I had some rough ideas about motives, but we needed more.

"I wonder if Trevor's had any luck with the security footage?"

She looked at her watch and grinned.

"Well, my shift doesn't start for another few hours and something tells me you can't focus on work, so let's go find out. It's been a while since I've been back in the security cave."

I put the marker down and nodded as I stowed the whiteboard away, out of sight. Maybe we'd luck out and Trevor would have the smoking gun that would give our boss a get out of jail free card. I flipped off the light and led Charlie down the hall. The door was propped open and I could see Trevor, lit with a blue glow from his screens. He was staring at something and tapping on his mouse.

"Hey Trev," Charlie said, flinging herself down in the chair across from his desk. "Whatcha got?"

He glanced up, tossed us a smile, before focusing back on his monitor.

"I've got something, but I'm not sure if it's going to be very helpful. Here," he said, rotating his monitor.

"What are we looking at?" Charlie said, leaning closer to squint at the grainy footage.

"This is the camera by the side door of the main building that exits to the east. See the timestamp? This is during the banquet, and before Rebecca's body was found. Someone definitely left and then came back during that time period."

"Yes!" I said, hopping a little. "But you don't seem very excited about it."

"Look closer," he said, tapping the edge of the screen. "You can't see their face. All we have is a figure wearing a winter coat, and they look pretty tall. This is one of our older cameras, so it's not in color and the quality is awful. It could literally be anyone. For all we know, it could be Marsburg and we're making it worse for him."

I sat down next to Charlie, deflated. I tapped my finger on the arm of the chair and thought for a second.

"Is there any way we could have someone do their Photoshop magic on it? I mean, there's got to be a way to enhance the image, right? Even if it's in black and white, we might narrow down the color of the coat, or something defining about the figure."

Trevor brightened and swung the screen back in his direction.

"You know what? I've got a buddy who's a graphic designer. Genius idea, Eden. I'll call him. It's a long shot, but you're right, we can't give up now."

He grabbed for his phone and we leaned forward as he punched in the number. I could hear it ringing before it went to voicemail. Trevor left a brief message and put his phone down.

"Now we wait. It might take a few hours."

"Eden, tell him about what you learned! You won't believe this Trev. She's got some major dirt on the ski team."

While we waited for Trevor's buddy to call back, I went through my experience in Kendra's room, leaving nothing out. I was just wrapping up my story when the hotel phone on Trevor's desk buzzed. He picked it up and put the call on speaker.

"What's up, Wendy?"

"Is Eden back there? I tried her office, but she didn't pick up."

"I'm here, Wendy."

"Could you come up to the front? Detective Rhodes is here."

I paled and nodded, forgetting Wendy couldn't see me. I took me a second to realize I should speak instead.

"I'll be right there."

Trevor hung up the phone and raised an eyebrow.

"What does he want?"

"I'm not sure, but I better go find out."

"Do you want me to come with you?" Charlie asked.

"I'll be fine. Let me know if your friend calls you back, Trevor."

I left them in his office and the short hallway to the lobby felt like it was miles long as I dragged my feet. What on earth was Ethan doing here?

Chapter Ten

W endy gave me a nervous smile as I walked up to the desk. Her eyes kept darting over to where Ethan stood at the windows, back to us, gazing out at the mountains in the distance. I skirted around the desk, bumping my hip on the edge. Ethan turned at the sound, in time to catch me grimacing as I rubbed the spot.

"Are you okay?"

"I'm fine. Just clumsy," I said, blushing so hard my cheeks felt like they were on fire.

Why was I always so awkward around this man? It never failed. I ignored the stabbing pain in my hip and tried to calm myself by taking a slow, deep breath. Hey, at least I didn't start choking. Progress, right?

"Is there somewhere we could talk?" Ethan asked, looking over my head towards Wendy.

She was focusing intently on the computer in front of her, but I knew darn well she wasn't looking at anything interesting. I couldn't blame her. We were all on pins and needles, waiting to hear what was going on with our boss. I nodded at Ethan and pointed to my left.

"Let's walk over here," I said, leading him towards the lounge area of the hotel.

He let out a low whistle as his eyes went up to the giant moose head mounted over the rock fireplace that went all the way to the top of the timbered ceiling. I wasn't a huge fan of dead critters, so I'd never looked closely at it.

"That must have been an enormous moose. I wonder where it was caught?"

"I'm not sure. I think it's been here since the lodge was built, back in the 1950s. Mr. Marsburg might know more about it."

We came to a stop at the furthest corner of the room, where two overstuffed leather chairs faced the windows, looking out to the pine forest. I motioned to the other chair while I sank into the one closest to me. And by that, I meant I literally sank down into its depths, legs kicked up in the air. I scooted forward, cheeks flaming again.

Ethan steepled his hands on top of his knees and looked at me, his sky-blue eyes sweeping over my face. His hair flopped down over his forehead and he impatiently brushed it to the side. I tore my eyes away, preferring to focus on the great outdoors.

"So, I..."

"I thought you..."

He gave me a wry smile at our overlapping words and motioned for me to speak first. My mouth picked that moment to feel as though I'd been trapped in the desert without water for days. I cleared my throat and shook my head.

"Go ahead."

"I thought you were going to leave the investigating to me," he said, eyes twinkling as he swept them over my face again. "I distinctly remember remarking about that last night."

I gripped my knees. What did he mean? I had done little, just talked to a few people on the ski team. How had it already gotten back to him? I made an inarticulate sound and shook my head.

"How did you? I mean, I don't know what you're talking about."

His lips curled up again, and he shook his head.

"Nice try. I got a call from Trent Jermain about an hour ago. Apparently, his daughter said someone from the hotel was harassing them and he wanted to file a formal complaint."

A bolt of pure indignation shot straight down to my toes and I nearly hopped out of the chair in a fury, barely checking myself. Jermain, Jermain. My mind raced through the names of the ski team members and settled on Sassy.

"What? I wasn't harassing them. I was checking to make sure they were okay, and it's not my fault if they had a big gossip session right in front of me. I barely said two words the entire time I was there."

"I told Mr. Jermain it was likely a misunderstanding and soothed his ruffled feathers. I thought I'd stop by and warn you to tread lightly around them. These people, Eden, they're used to being the top dog no matter where they go. They don't care who they step on along the way. I'm not asking you to stop poking your nose into this case. I know that's impossible. I'm just telling you to be careful."

I blinked in surprise at his gentle tone. He wouldn't hassle me about investigating? Had I woken up in an alternate reality? I tilted my head to the side and looked at him in a new light.

"You don't mind?"

"I didn't say that," he said, grinning lopsidedly before brushing his hair off his forehead again. "I mind, but I think I understand the way your brain works."

I didn't know how to take that and I shifted in my chair. Did I want Ethan Rhodes to know the way my brain worked? For once, I was completely speechless. He started talking again as he looked back outside.

"You're a fair person, and the way you see the world intrigues me. I wish I had your innocence. You've got good instincts. You proved that with Emma and the Youngstowns. It made me think about the way I approach my cases."

My hand came up to my chest as he spoke.

"So you agree with me that Marsburg is innocent? Why did you take him in?"

The smile slid off his face, and he shook his head.

"I didn't say that. There are... inconsistencies that are making me hesitant to rush to judgment."

I waited for him, hoping he'd fill in some blanks, but he fell quiet, looking out the window with a pensive expression.

"Inconsistencies?"

"A few. You know I can't go into details, Eden, although I wish I could. You've got a keen mind, and it's nice to share theories with someone else. I'm the only detective in Valewood, and the chief isn't one for spit balling sessions. He prefers everything cut and dried, and making the wealthy townspeople happy."

I sifted through what he wasn't saying and understanding dawned.

"You're under pressure from the Yardleys to solve this quickly. Marsburg, given his prior relationship with Rebecca, and that their engagement ring was found in the snow, makes it look bad for him."

He raised an eyebrow as I spoke, but I waved him off before continuing.

"I found a picture of them and recognized the ring you showed me. The only thing is motive, Ethan. I don't see what he had to gain from killing her. She was engaged to Ash, but she was planning on breaking it off. So, I don't think Marsburg flew into a fit of violent rage at the news of her engagement. I just wish I knew why that ring was in the snow and the new one was still on her finger."

He scooted forward in his chair, his knees brushing mine.

"What did you just say?"

"About the ring in the snow?"

"No, about her engagement. She was going to break it off?"

"That's what I overheard this morning. I think it was Sassy who said Rebecca found out about Ash and a snow bunny and she was ready to end it. If you ask me, Ash is the one with the motive, although he's not the only one. Thanks to their relationship, he was due to join her father's firm and if she ended the engagement, that opportunity would be gone."

"Not the only one? What do you mean? From the interviews last night, it seemed like she was universally loved."

"Well, that's not the vibe I got from them this morning. Alicia idolized her. But Sassy and Kendra were dripping vitriol all over the place this morning. The entire team was more upset that the competition might be canceled than by her death. I may be sheltered, but I know ambition and rank jealousy when I see it. I'm not pointing a finger at them yet, but I think it's a lead worth pursuing."

Ethan nodded, and his hair flopped onto his forehead again. He brushed it back impatiently.

"Interesting. What else did you hear?"

"Alicia mentioned Kendra was the one who'd likely take Rebecca's place in the slalom, but Sassy was also in the running. There's a lot of infighting. They certainly had more motive than Marsburg."

"Eden, I know you want to support your boss, and I appreciate that. But he was outside with her, by his own admission."

"The security footage," I said, sitting up straighter. "Trevor's working on it right now. There's another camera that spotted someone going out a side door, around the time Rebecca was outside. It's not great footage, but he's going to see if he can get a buddy to enhance it."

Ethan's face sobered, and he stood, hands on hips.

"What? Why wasn't I shown this footage last night?"

I slid back in my chair involuntarily at his loud tone before I caught myself. I gripped the arms of the chair and moved back.

"It was something we thought of this morning. The camera at the banquet doors was only one view, and Rebecca couldn't be seen. Why couldn't someone have snuck out another door and doubled back to the patio area, out of sight? And it looks like that's exactly what happened. We were going to improve the footage and see who it was."

Ethan flushed, and his eyebrows furrowed into an angry line.

"That evidence needs to be shared with my department. We have access to people who do that for a living, without breaking the chain of evidence."

He spun on his heel and marched out of the lounge area. I struggled to get out of the chair and hurried after him.

"Ethan, wait."

He kept walking as I panted in my effort to catch up with him.

"I'm sorry, Ethan. We weren't trying to do anything wrong. We were trying to help."

He ground to a halt in the lobby, where Wendy was staring at us, eyes huge. His eyes closed as he took a deep breath through his nose, the sound loud in the lobby's quiet atmosphere.

"I know that. But you aren't professionals. I am. This is my job. All the footage should've been turned over last night. Now, it may not be admissible in court. Look, Eden, I appreciate what you're doing. I know it's part of who you are, but in a case like this, everything, and I mean, everything, has to be done properly. You can overhear damning remarks, but it's up to me to sift through the hearsay, interview each person, and build my case. You don't know the people we're dealing with. Do you know how easy it would be for them to say Trevor hired a friend to manipulate the footage to shift the blame off your boss onto someone else?"

An exasperated noise burst out of his chest as he continued down the hall to the security office. I bit my lip as tears threatened. He was absolutely right. I felt about two inches tall as Wendy gave me a sympathetic look.

I stood for a second, trying to figure out what to do as Charlie came out of the hallway, her face pale. She opened her mouth, and I shook my head, holding up a hand.

"We'd better not say anything," I said, looking over her shoulder.

She hustled around the desk and put an arm around my shoulders, leading me outside. I hesitated, knowing I had work to do, but I was unwilling to go down the hallway to my office for fear of running into Ethan.

"No, let's go to your cabin. You can come back later," she said, looking back over her shoulder. "Okay, the doors are shut. What on earth happened? Ethan came running into Trevor's office like his hair was on fire."

I stopped and looked at the doors, half dreading Ethan was going to burst through them and rake me over the coals again. Which I deserved. I hung my head, miserable.

"I mentioned the footage we found. I didn't even think about it. We could make things worse for Marsburg, instead of better. I'm an idiot."

"Hey! Don't you say that about my friend in front of me," Charlie said, poking a finger into my shoulder. "Nobody talks about Eden Brooks that way. Not in my hearing."

Her face looked fierce as she grabbed my arms.

"Your heart was in the right place, Eden, and I'm sure Ethan knows that. Once he gets over his snit, he'll realize that and thank you for what you found. Why was he here, anyway? Did he say what's going on with our boss?"

I shook my head and stepped back, breaking her hold.

"No, just that his chief wants things wrapped up, and he's apparently dealing with a lot of powerful people. He's here because Sassy Jermain complained to her father I was harassing them. I just want to go back to my cabin, Charlie."

"That little wretch. Harassing? I'll show her harassing!"

She turned and shook her fist at the windows of the hotel, and a tiny smile played on my lips at her outraged expression.

"It's okay. I'm not in trouble or anything. Well, I wasn't, until I mentioned the footage. Why wasn't that handed over?"

"I'm sure he did, but there's too much to go through. It's not your fault you had the idea of looking at the other cameras. In fact, Ethan should thank you for your insight. I'm sure he will once he pulls his head out of his..."

"Charlie!"

"Well, I don't like anyone yelling at you. Come on, let's get you back to your cabin and you can cuddle with Jasper, take a nap, and forget about all of this for today. I need to get ready to go back to work, but you need to take some time off, Eden. It's just too much."

I followed her, numb, knowing full well there was zero chance of me taking a nap. Not right now. No, my plans involved doing a little research on my laptop and calling Hannah Murphy. I wasn't about to quit my investigation, no matter how many times Ethan yelled at me. He might have been right about the chain of evidence, but I knew Marsburg was innocent. There was no way I was going to stand back and let him get railroaded by the rich and powerful, even they were his peers. I glanced back at the hotel and nodded sharply, as if Ethan could see me.

Chapter Eleven

P acing back and forth while my laptop fired up accomplished little, but it made me feel better, so it had to count for something, right? Jasper watched me, his eyes flicking back and forth as I silently walked back and forth. How long was this computer going to take?

"Oh my gosh, now it needs to update," I said, throwing my hands in the air. "Why does it never do this when I'm not in a hurry?"

"Why don't you call Hannah while you're waiting?"

I flopped on the bed, making Jasper bounce. I immediately put my hand on his back.

"I'm sorry! I didn't mean to jostle you. Great idea, though. I'll call her."

"I'm not made of china, I'll be fine."

He sat up, his golden eyes gleaming, while I dialed Hannah's number. I wasn't sure what she'd be doing, but I could only hope she had a few minutes to spare. Hearing her bright voice through the line suddenly put me at ease.

"Eden! I was just thinking about you this morning. How are things at the resort?"

"Um, well, they were going great until yesterday. Have you heard anything?"

"No, but I've had my head buried in finishing up a story about a spy ring."

"A what now? In Golden Hills?"

"It's a long story," she said with a sigh. "I have a feeling you've got something going on. What's up?"

"Is that Eden? I want to talk to Jasper."

Hearing that familiar sweet voice eased a little more of the ache in my chest. Jasper's ears perked up as he caught his name, and he leaned closer to the phone.

"Razzy?"

"Hi, Jasper! Oh, I'm so glad you're with Eden. We heard about the terrible cold snap and I was worried about you."

If a cat could blush, Jasper's cheeks would've been flame red. He cleared his throat awkwardly and bobbed his head.

"I'm fine. How's that young whippersnapper?"

"Hey, Jasper. This is Rudy. Callie's going to be so relieved. She's been really upset. Is everyone in the clowder okay? She sends her love."

Rudy's piping voice was going a mile a minute, and I watched as Jasper shook his head fondly.

"They'll be fine. Fig's doing a great job. Luna's expecting some kits."

A deep voice came on the line and I nearly jumped.

"In this season?"

"Ah, Gus, I recognize your voice. Yes, Luna and Oscar are expecting. I think it will be a few more weeks. You know from your experience it's not ideal, but there's no reasoning with those two."

I could hear a tussle on the other end and could almost see Razzy pushing her way to the phone.

"We miss you, Eden. You too, Jasper. Are you going to visit us soon?"

"Ask him if they've ever seen any aliens in the woods. That would be a great place to see some," Rudy said.

"Okay, guys, that's enough. Eden just started her job. We can't expect her to take a vacation at the drop of a hat. It sounds like she's got her hands full," Hannah said, her tone wry.

"Well, we could go see her. Bye, Eden."

A chorus of byes from the other two cats drowned out Razzy's muttering and I swallowed a smile, imagining the look on her expressive little face. There was no cat quite like Razzy. Jasper curled back up, tucking his paws underneath his chest, a little kitty smile on his face.

"Sorry about that. They're still wound up from the past week. And no, Rudy, I'm not asking again about aliens. We've talked about that."

"Do I want to know?" I asked, finally unable to restrain my laughter.

"No. You definitely don't. Trust me. Where were we?"

"There's been another murder here."

"Again?" Hannah asked, her voice ratcheting up a few octaves.

"Yeah. I couldn't believe it. This is bad, though, Hannah. Ethan took our boss in and we're all worried he's going to be locked up."

"James Marsburg is a good man. And Ethan's a good cop. There must be a reason he wanted to question him."

"Do you think Ben could find out what's going on?"

Ben Walsh, Hannah's boyfriend, was a detective in Golden Hills, and he'd become friendly with Ethan during an investigation. I knew it was a long shot, but Ben had helped me before and I wasn't too shy to ask if he'd mind again. Hannah's long silence told me I might be wrong about that, though.

"Ben's no longer with the department. He's going to go out on his own as a private investigator. I'll ask him, though."

If I hadn't been seated, I would've fallen over. I blinked at the phone, trying to make sense of what I'd just heard.

"Is everything okay? Do you need anything?"

"We're fine. Honestly, it's the best thing that could've happened. Back to the murder, though. Start at the beginning."

I shook off my worry for Ben and Hannah. With the two of their investigative instincts combined, I had a feeling he was going to be a very successful PI. I took a long breath and jumped right in, telling Hannah everything I knew. She listened quietly, although I could hear the occasional gasp from the cats as they listened in.

"Wow, that is intense. Do you know Ash's last name? I've been jotting everything down and I'd be happy to run some of these names for you."

I slapped my hand to my forehead and groaned. I hadn't been able to ask the ski team during their gossip session, but Wendy might know.

"I don't, but I can find out. Hannah, do you think I'm grasping at straws? That I'm seeing suspects where there aren't just because I'm worried about losing my job if my boss is guilty?"

There it was. I laid out my biggest fear and waited, holding my breath for her answer.

Hannah Murphy was one of the best people I knew. Her kindness was honest. She'd always tell you the truth, even if it was difficult to hear. She was quiet for a moment, and my heart clenched painfully.

"Based on what I know about my interactions with Marsburg, and from what you've said, I think you're right. My gut says he's innocent. He just doesn't have a motive, especially if it's true Rebecca was going to cut ties with Ash. The soon to be ex-fiance is the one with the strongest motive. It sounds like he had plenty to lose if she kicked him to the curb."

Relief flooded through me at her words and I nodded enthusiastically, even though she couldn't see me.

"Oh, thank you, Hannah. I was so worried."

"Trust your instincts. They're solid. I'll do some research after I finish what I'm working on and see what I can dig up. I have a feeling I've got three little helpers who'll want to pitch in, too."

A chorus of agreement in the background made me smile. If anyone knew our secret about cats talking and using computers, they'd probably have us committed. I glanced at my little investigative assistant and gave him a thumbs up. Jasper flicked an ear and reached a paw out to pat my foot.

"I really appreciate it, Hannah. I'll do some searching, too. I'll text you if I find anything."

"Back at you. Stay safe, Eden. It sounds like the murderer could still be around."

"I'll be fine. Kisses to your sweet kitties."

"And a big hug to Jasper," Hannah said, the smile clear in her voice. "We'll talk soon."

I ended the call and hugged my knees to my chest. I didn't know what it was about Hannah, but she always knew what to say. I slid my laptop over and propped it on my lap.

"Alright, Jasper. Let's see what we can find out."

He perked up and rose, stretching, before sitting next to me where he could see the screen. It hadn't taken him long to become interested in technology. Before long, I might need to get him a little tablet like Razzy and her friends.

I started with Rebecca's name, typing it into the search bar to see what would come up. Beyond the fact she was on the ski team, and from a wealthy family, I knew little about her. The first search result was a news story from a few weeks ago, when she'd won a competition with her team. I clicked on it and settled back to read.

"Look, Jasper, in this picture," I said, swiveling the screen towards him. "Ashland Billingsley the Third. That's him!"

"Hmph. He looks like a tool."

I bit my lip to keep from laughing. He wasn't wrong. Ashland was definitely full of himself. His white teeth gleamed in the picture. He had his arm around Rebecca, and even though she was the one who'd won, the camera seemed to focus on him. I quickly texted Hannah his name and flipped back to my search, entering his name into the bar.

There wasn't much that came back. He'd gone to a local university and had graduated with a law degree the year before. He and his parents were apparently prominent philanthropists. I wrinkled my forehead as I continued to flip back and forth, reading about him, before pushing the laptop to the side in frustration.

"Well, from all of that, you'd think Ash was a saint," Jasper said, bending to lick a paw. "But something doesn't smell right to me. He's too perfect."

"Can I get you something to eat? I think I'll just stay here tonight. I don't feel like going to the dining hall."

He perked up and beat me over to the kitchenette, hopping onto the counter with an ease that belied his years.

"Do we have any of that beef stuff? That was pretty good."

I smoothed the fur on his back as I nodded, turning to grab the packets I'd bought the week before. He'd been a big fan of this food and I made a note to stock up on it.

"Of course."

Once he was face first into his bowl, enthusiastically slurping up the gravy, I turned to my fridge as my mind wandered. Was Ash too obvious a choice? He had his own power and prestige. He didn't really need to be allied with the Yardleys. Unless there was more to his background that I wasn't finding. I shook my head and realized I'd been standing there with the door open for far too long. I grabbed a container of leftovers, some lettuce, and closed the fridge, and headed back to the counter.

The savory smell of lasagna warming in the microwave filled my cabin as I shredded up the lettuce to make a salad. The food at the resort was top-notch, and I still couldn't believe they didn't mind if you took leftovers with you from the dining hall. Before long, I'd finished my meal, done the dishes and was snuggled back into bed with Jasper, continuing our research.

I worked for a few more hours, taking notes on a pad of paper as I learned more about the ski team. I'd ended up going down several dead-ends, but just as I was about to give up for the night, I saw something that made me sit up straight.

"Jasper!"

He stopped bathing, little pink tongue hanging out of his mouth, and turned to me, startled.

"What?"

"Listen to this! Kendra Baldwin used to be on a different ski team, down in the southern part of the state. According to this message board, she was asked to leave when there were questions about how one of her teammates ended up injured."

"Are you saying she intentionally got someone hurt?"

I nodded, rubbing my eyes. I'd been staring at the screen for far too long.

"It looks like it. I'll need to confirm it, though. I'm not sure this message board full of gossip is an excellent source."

He looked doubtful, but gave a kitty shrug and curled into a ball.

"Why don't you call it a night? You've been going over that for hours. It may make more sense in the morning."

I glanced at the clock on my bedside table and my eyes flared open. Holy smokes, it was nearly midnight. I snapped the laptop shut and crawled out of bed, stiff from sitting in the same position for too long.

"Good idea. I'll be just a second."

I hurried through my nightly routine and slid back under the warm covers. Jasper eased closer to me as I flipped off the light. I'd learned quite a few things, but it felt like I was missing something. Something big. I huffed out a sigh and turned over on my side, determined to put it out of my head and get some sleep.

Chapter Twelve

I t was still dark when I came awake to Jasper's hiss. I rolled over, head spinning, and tried to focus. Jasper was sitting bolt upright, fur fluffed, and a low growl was coming from his chest. I reached for him, but he ducked out of the way and stood over me, his growl even louder.

"What is it? What's wrong?"

"There's someone here. They're right outside. Don't move. Don't speak."

Fear propelled me upward and for a second, I thought my heart was going to pound out of my chest. I tried to listen, but all I could hear was the thumping going on inside my chest. I froze, terrified, my hands forming into fists underneath the covers. Who would be outside by cabin at this hour? A loud bang came from my door and I nearly came out of my skin, a shout of terror barely staying inside my chest.

I could hear footsteps crunching through the snow. I waited as the sound receded, and the only thing I could hear was my panicked breathing.

Finally, fraction by fraction, Jasper's posture relaxed. It was then

I noticed how shaky he was as he sat back, his puffed up fur slowly going back down.

"Jasper, are you okay?"

I could just make out the gleam in his eyes as they blinked at me. He licked the fur on his chest before answering me.

"I'm fine. They're gone. I haven't felt that kind of intent in years."

I was slowly easing my legs from under the comforter and stopped as his words sunk in. "You can feel intent? What do you mean?"

"You know how people always say animals know who the good people are? It's because we feel it, down to our whiskers. Whoever was outside that door was not a good person, Eden. They felt black, down to their soul."

I didn't know what to say, but I stared at the door as if answers would magically appear on its wooden surface. What had that bang meant? I put my feet on the floor and groped around for my slippers.

"You're sure they're gone?" I asked, wringing my hands together as I stood.

Jasper jumped down from the bed and strode towards the door, his tail lashing back and forth. He lowered his head to the bottom of the door and went still, his ears swiveling in the darkness.

"They're gone. You can turn on the light if you need it. I know you can't see as well in the dark as I can."

I immediately flipped on my bedside lamp and the warm glow it cast around the cabin eased the grip of fear from around my heart. I slowly walked over to join Jasper and put my hand on the door. It had been long enough I knew there was little chance of catching sight of whoever had been at the door, but it was difficult to force my hand to turn the knob.

Jasper's warm fur brushed my ankle, giving me courage, and I swung the door open, sticking my head out to look around. No one was in sight. My shoulders slumped, and I took a small step forward. The glow to the eastern horizon meant sunrise wasn't far off, but everything was frozen in a hushed silence. My lungs ached as I took a deep breath of the frosty morning air.

"You're right, Jasper. They're gone. You can see the footprints, though. Whoever was here had some enormous feet."

He carefully picked his way forward, avoiding the prints, and sniffed.

"It was a man. I don't recognize the scent. Whoever it was, they don't work here at the resort."

I crossed my arms over my chest and rubbed them. It was freezing out here. I turned to go back inside and stopped, my mouth falling open. There, right in the middle of my door, was a note, held in place by a wicked-looking knife. My hand reached for the paper almost without my realizing it, but I stopped at Jasper's warning hiss.

"Don't touch it!"

It was dark enough that the faint light from my lamp didn't illuminate the writing. I leaned back to flip on the overhead light and gasped as I read the words. Fear twisted through my stomach.

"Get inside, Jasper."

I closed the door as soon as the tip of his tail was through it and backed away once I'd relocked it. I grabbed my phone from the bed table and stared at it. I knew who I needed to call, even though I really didn't want to talk to him.

"You have to call him. This is serious."

"I know. I know."

I found Ethan's number in my contacts and took a deep breath before hitting the phone icon. He answered on the second ring.

"Eden, what's wrong? Are you okay?"

I stammered for a second, startled by his greeting. It took me a second, and I breathed in through my nose to calm down.

"I'm okay, but someone put something on the door of my cabin. It's probably just a joke or something. I probably shouldn't have called. I'm so sorry to bother you..."

"I'll be there in ten minutes. Is your door locked?"

"Yes. I'm safe."

"Don't leave your cabin. I'll be right there."

He ended the call, leaving me staring at my phone, looking at his contact card. I slowly put the phone aside and looked down at my fuzzy pajama pants. Right. I needed to get changed. I walked to the bathroom to wash my face and brush my teeth. I looked at my reflection in the mirror and winced. I didn't like the look I saw in my eyes. I avoided the mirror while I finished getting ready.

Once I was dressed, I made my bed and sat on it with Jasper. He leaned into me, and I stroked his head, deep in thought. Had I over-reacted? The note was probably a joke, right? My phone rang, breaking into my thoughts, and Ethan's name flashed on the screen.

"Eden, I'm approaching your cabin now. I can see your lights. A patrol car was following me. They'll be here shortly."

Oh gosh, everyone was going to know what was going on before long. Doubt crept back in, and I shook my head.

"It's probably nothing. I'm so sorry for causing all this hassle."

"Eden, stop. I'm a few feet away. If you come to your window, you'll be able to see me."

His kind voice broke through my self recriminations and I walked to the window, spotting him just a short distance away. He waved, and I waved back, feeling slightly silly.

"He's here," I said, even though I knew Jasper already knew that.

He nodded and stared at the door from his spot on the bed. I looked back out the window and saw Ethan taking a picture of my door and the ground right in front of it. A hollow sound came through the door, and I realized he must have pulled the knife out. The sick feeling was back in my stomach as I remembered the length of the blade.

"Eden? You can open the door."

I rushed over to it and swung it wide. There was a gash in the wood where the knife had been. I stared at it for a second before motioning Ethan to come inside. He was carrying a big plastic bag with the knife and the note.

"Thanks for coming," I said, stepping back and putting my hands in my pockets. "I'm sorry to pull you out of bed so early."

"It's fine," he said, eyes searching mine. "Are you sure you're okay? Can you describe what happened?"

I nodded and looked over at Jasper.

"I was sound asleep when I heard Jasper hiss. He said... I mean, he growled as he stood over me, and I sat up, trying to figure out what was going on. I heard a loud noise, which I guess must have been the knife. I waited for a few minutes to make sure they were gone before I went to the door."

I'd almost revealed Jasper's communications skills, but I'd caught myself just in time. If Ethan noticed anything odd about what I'd said, he didn't show it. Instead, he walked over to the bed and gently patted Jasper's head.

"Good kitty. I'm glad you protected her," he said, his expression sobering as he turned back to look at me. "Did you read the note?"

I nodded and wrapped my arms around my waist, inadvertently shivering.

"I'm sure it's probably a joke or something, right?"

"Threatening to slit your throat if you keep poking your nose around is hardly a laughing matter, Eden. This is very serious. Do you have somewhere else you can stay? Any family you can go to?"

I shook my head so hard my braid swung over my shoulder. I mean, yes, I had family, but they lived hours away and there was no way I was welcome. Even if I'd wanted to stay with them, that wasn't an option. Not anymore. That bridge was burned the minute I walked out of that door a few years ago, intent on breaking free and starting my life over..

"No, but I'm sure I'll be fine."

He was quiet, hands on hips, as he stared at me.

"I don't like it. Can you bunk with that other girl? What's her name?"

"Charlie? I mean, yeah, I guess we could do that. Do you think that's really necessary? I don't want to make a big scene out of this."

I turned away, in time to spot the red and blue lights flashing in the parking lot. It was too late for that. Everyone at the resort was about to know what happened.

"It's very necessary. I can't stress how much danger you might be in. Can you tell me who you've talked to recently? Is there anyone at the resort who would do this?"

"No," I said, pausing for a second to think about Penny before shaking my head. This wasn't her style. "No, it's no one who works here. I guess that leaves the guests. You already know about my talk with the ski team members."

I looked at him meaningfully. Now that my brain was working, I was putting together the pieces and from where I was standing, with a hole in my door that used to hold a knife, it was pretty clear that Rebecca's murderer was on the loose and likely staying just a few hundred feet away.

"Yes, it's likely that whoever did this is staying here, which is why it's important that you're never alone. Whether this is directly related to the person who killed Rebecca needs to be determined. It could be someone who doesn't appreciate you casting doubt on their integrity."

I screwed up my lips and glared at him.

"Well, one thing is for sure, Mr. Marsburg isn't the one who left this. Is he still in custody?"

Ethan shook his head, and his bangs flopped over his forehead. He brushed them aside impatiently.

"He never was in custody, Eden. I questioned him for a few hours yesterday. We don't have enough to hold him, much to the chief's chagrin. He's out."

Well, that took the wind out of my sails. Burst of triumph fading, I started pacing.

"It's got to be someone on the ski team, Ethan. It has to be. Or the fiance. Did you know Kendra had to leave her old ski team when one of her teammates was injured? So, whomever was on that security feed is likely the same person who did this, right?"

He straightened as I mentioned the security footage and dropped his head down.

"I owe you an apology for my behavior yesterday. That footage was handed over. We just hadn't gone through it yet. Our team's working on it now. But what I said still stands, Eden. You've got to let us do our job. I appreciate your help, honestly I do, but look what happened. It's not safe, you've got to realize that. I'd rather have someone come after me. At least I'm trained to protect myself. I can't stand to think of you being out here alone, at the mercy of someone who's already killed once and might do so again."

"But Rebecca was strangled. Not knifed."

He let out an angry sigh and shook his head.

"It doesn't matter. If you won't leave the resort, promise me you won't stay here alone. I'm going to post one of our cars here. We'll rotate shifts."

I couldn't promise that. If someone was always with me, that meant I wouldn't be able to talk to Jasper, or go see the clowder cats.

"I'll stay safe," I said, skirting the whole promise thing. "I won't talk to anyone on the ski team, unless it's for official hotel business."

His beautiful blue eyes narrowed and his freckles stood out on his pale face. He knew darn well what I wasn't saying.

"Are any of these cabins vacant?" he asked, motioning outside.

"Um, maybe? I don't know. Why?"

He nodded and gave Jasper another pat before walking towards the door.

"I need to log this evidence. The officer outside will dust the door for prints and we'll run these, but there's a chance we won't get anything usable. Until we catch this person, please check in with people you trust throughout the day. That includes me, Eden. I want a text whenever you go anywhere and another one when you arrive. This is serious."

I sputtered as he opened the door, turning to face me. He looked into my eyes, holding them captive.

"You can trust me, Eden. I want you safe."

And with that, he turned, closing the door behind him. I glared at the door before turning to Jasper, who was still on the bed.

"He's got you tied up right and tight, doesn't he? Well, I have to admit, he's a smart one. I approve. He's got your best interests at heart," he said, curling into a ball and wrapping his tail around his muzzle.

My eyes narrowed to slits as I turned to stare at the door. Jasper was right. Ethan had maneuvered me right into a corner. What had he meant about the cabins? I looked at my watch and sighed. It looked like I was going to work early, and if I found the time to do a little more research, so be it. No matter how unsettling that note was, the killer was still out there and I refused to let fear rule me.

Chapter Thirteen

J asper curled up, content in bed, and I looked over my shoulder as I left, wishing I could go back to bed, too. As I walked to the main building, I spotted the patrol car, still in our parking lot, a man at the wheel. I hunched my shoulders down inside my coat and walked into the lobby, stamping the snow off my boots.

"You are in big trouble."

I met Charlie's eyes and winced as she rounded the desk, stomping in my direction. I should've called her, but in all fairness, I was still in shock over discovering a knife buried in my door. Yeah, I know, no excuses. Charlie was my best friend.

"I'm sorry," I said, keeping my eyes down. "I was going to call, but then I figured I'd just deliver the bad news in person."

She flung her arms around me, smooshing my puffy coat down as she gripped me.

"I just want to make sure you're alright. Now, tell me what happened. Why is the fuzz still sitting in our parking lot, even though Ethan left a few minutes ago?"

I peeled off my coat as I told her what happened, and her eyes grew wide as I described the knife.

"Oh my gosh, Eden. That's super serious. I knew something was off when Ethan walked in and started asking if I'd seen anyone and wouldn't answer any of my questions. From the look on his face, I knew it had to be something going on with you."

"What do you mean?" I asked as I pulled off my stocking hat and smoothed my staticky hair.

"He gets this super serious look when you're in danger. But Eden, no one came through the lobby. You can see pretty well outside, and I don't think anyone was in the parking lot, but it's not like I had my eyes trained on it the whole time. How did they make it over to your cabin?"

"I suppose they might have parked on the road and come through the woods, but that doesn't seem likely. I guess if they came from this building, they might have used a side exit. Is there a way to pull a record of the keycards that have been used at the doors?"

Charlie cracked her gum absently while she thought and shook her head.

"I don't think so. But we should ask Trevor when he gets in. Are you sure you're okay? If I was in your shoes. I'd be hiding in my bed with the covers pulled over my head.

"I'm fine. Right now, I don't want to think about it. The important thing is, whoever it was didn't break in. They just wanted to scare me. And they succeeded."

Charlie's face furrowed, and she rubbed my arm.

"Well, I'm going to stick to you like glue."

I noticed she stifled a yawn and shook my head.

"You've got to sleep sometime, Charlie. I'll be fine. People who do that get off on the scare. I don't think they'd have the guts to actually do something."

As I spoke, I willed myself to believe it. It sounded good, but I had no clue if it was anywhere close to being accurate. From the dubious look Charlie was giving me, she didn't buy it either.

"O-kay," she said, heading back behind the desk as I walked towards the hall to my office. "Oh, Marsburg's back. He's not in a good mood, though, so I'd avoid him. I didn't know what to say when he walked in an hour ago. He just nodded and blew right past me."

My steps faltered, and I spun around to look at her.

"Mr. Marsburg got here an hour ago?"

"Yeah. I told Ethan that, and he went back to talk to him before he left."

The hotel phone rang and Charlie made a face before turning to answer it. Doubts swirled around as I walked back towards my office. Would he be the type to do something like leaving an awful note pinned with a knife to my door? I didn't think so. I had almost made it past his door when he called out my name.

"Eden? Why are you here so early? You're not due for another couple of hours."

So much for being sneaky. I popped my head into his office and tried to smile.

"I was awakened early and couldn't get back to sleep, so I figured I'd come in and get some work done."

"Well, I don't want you overworking yourself," he said, his handsome face lined with fatigue. "Make sure you leave early, okay?"

I nodded and tried to figure out a tactful way to ask my boss how his questioning at the police department went. I came up empty and just went for it.

"Is everything okay? I mean with the..."

I trailed off miserably, and he motioned for me to come in and take a seat. He leaned back in his chair and looked out the window.

"Detective Rhodes mentioned you'd been investigating on your own, and I appreciate it, Eden. It's funny how people treat you differently when you're under suspicion for something so heinous. Even Diane isn't one hundred percent certain. I am innocent, but I'll admit it looks bad."

"Because of the ring?"

He turned towards me, his eyes more deeply lined than I'd ever seen them, and nodded his head slowly.

"Because of the ring. Rhodes wasn't kidding when he said you were thorough. Rebecca kept it when we ended things. I insisted on it. It had been designed especially for her, and there was no way I was going to sell it or, God forbid, give it to another woman should that occasion ever arise. It was hers, no matter what happened between us. I didn't know she still wore it, though. I was shocked when Rhodes said it was found in the snow by her body."

I scooted forward in my chair.

"Was she wearing it that night? I never saw her since we got to the banquet a little late."

"She was," he said, nodding. "She always wore it, just on her other hand. She called me a few days before they came, wanting advice."

"About what to do with Ash?"

One eyebrow went up as he made eye contact with me.

"You are well informed. Yes, because of Ash. I warned her about his reputation when they got together, but she swore he was faithful. I felt like an old stick, so I let it go. I wanted what was best for her and I knew in my soul it wasn't Ash."

"Do you think he's the one?"

Marsburg looked back out the window and shrugged.

"I don't know. I've been wracking my brain trying to figure out who would want to snuff out a light as bright as Rebecca. I wasn't holding a torch for her," he said, one side of his mouth curling up. "I knew it wouldn't work between us, even if it took me a few months to agree with her. She was an amazing woman, and this world is a colder place without her in it."

I didn't know what to say. He hadn't mentioned the note on my door, so I had to assume Ethan hadn't mentioned it to him, which was strange. Curiosity made me bold.

"Charlie mentioned Detective Rhodes came back here a little while ago. What did he want?"

He levered back up to sit at his desk and shook his head slightly.

"He wanted to see my boots, which was strange, but I obliged him. He also mentioned posting a patrol car in the parking lot, which I encouraged, as well as a few other safety measures. Rebecca's murderer is still out there, and if they're staying in this hotel, I want them found. You and the other women are taking precautions, right? I've been so tied up, I feel like I've let things slide here."

"We are," I said, smiling as the shadow of doubt I'd had about him faded completely. "We're also doing our best to find the killer. We found some security footage that might help the case."

He turned towards the credenza behind his desk and looked at the photo of him and Rebecca, now back in an upright position.

"I appreciate it, Eden. It's good to know my staff didn't think the worst of me, even if the people who know me better did."

"Oh, no, sir. We never doubted your innocence, and we'd do whatever it took to find the proof to back that up."

He nodded, clearly absorbed in the photo, and I stood, walking over to the door. I hovered in the doorway and he finally spoke.

"Her memorial service will be in a few days. I hope Diane and Rob senior will allow me to attend. I still can't believe she's gone."

"I'm sorry, Mr. Marsburg. I hope her killer is found quickly."

"That makes two of us."

He said nothing else, and I left him, staring at the photo as I walked the few steps to my office and flipped on the light. Everything was as I'd left it, and I let out a sigh of relief. In the back of my mind, I'd half expected to find another threatening note sitting on my desk, or worse, impaled on it. I slid into my chair and booted up my computer, drumming my fingers on my desk as I waited for it to come to life.

Ethan obviously wanted to see if Marsburg had tramped through the snow to get to my cabin, and he must have been satisfied he hadn't. But his lack of sharing what took place on the property Marsburg owned still meant he wasn't certain Marsburg was innocent. I stared at my screen before remembering the whiteboard I'd tucked between my filing cabinet and desk. I leaned down to pull it out and propped it up behind me, lost in thought.

Ash was definitely a suspect, but I still couldn't find a powerful motive to link him to the crime. He'd been present, but so had every member of the ski team. I closed my eyes and tried to picture the night of the banquet in my head. I still couldn't place Kendra there, even though everyone said she attended. Sam was also someone I hadn't met yet. His motive was questionable, but still worth exploring.

My mind kept going over the possibilities, rejecting some, and clinging to others. I scribbled on the whiteboard so I wouldn't forget anything before realizing what I was doing. Even though I'd been warned, and hideously, I still wanted to move forward. After talking with Marsburg, I was even more motivated to find out who killed Rebecca and cleared his name.

I grabbed a notepad and made some notes on who I still needed to interview before realizing I'd never actually talked with their coach. If I was looking for more information on the members of the ski team, who better to ask than Christian St. John?

I put the whiteboard back into its hiding place and slid the notepad into my bag. Luckily, I knew Charlie would be more than happy to let me know where I could find the coach. I looked at my computer and winced, realizing I still wasn't getting much actual work done. I shook my head as I stood. Right now, this was way more important. I flipped off my light and headed for the front desk, noticing my boss's door was shut. The lights were off, so he must have left. I kept moving and found Charlie sitting at the desk, holding a book out of sight.

"Hey, Charlie!"

She jumped and quickly hid her book before realizing it was me.

"Geez, Louise. You scared the crap out of me. What's up? I just saw Marsburg leave. He seemed a little better. Did you talk to him?"

I waved my hand, nodding.

"Yes, but that's not important right now. Have you seen St. John anywhere? I still need to talk to him before it's too late."

Charlie's eyebrows winged up, and she tilted her head to the side.

"I have, but why? What are you up to?"

"I still think Rebecca's killer is on that team. He might have the insight we're missing. Where did you see him?"

"He went for a run about a half hour ago. Outside. Can you believe it? It's almost below zero out there."

"Oh."

My heart sank as I looked out onto the snowy landscape. I was not a runner, even in the best weather, but if I wanted a chance to grab the coach when the rest of the team wasn't around, this looked like the best opportunity.

I pulled my hat on and shrugged into my coat while Charlie shook her head.

"You are dedicated. Are you sure it's safe for you to be traipsing around out there? It's been pretty slow. I can go with you."

"I'll be fine. I'm just going to see if I can spot him. With any luck, he's on his way back and I can talk to him right here."

She shook her head as I marched to the front door. I wouldn't let cold air stop me from a chance to talk to St. John, alone with not a ski team member in sight. I huddled inside my coat as a blast of cold air quickly made me doubt myself. I shook it off and looked around, finally spotting someone in a bright blue parka jogging near the snowy treeline. Bingo! I headed in that direction, waving to the officer in the parking lot as I went.

Chapter Fourteen

My nose felt like it needed to move to another person's face, preferably someone who lived somewhere tropical, by the time I caught up with Christian St. John. Of all the days to forget my scarf, it had to be this one. I waved as he approached, and he slowed his jog, head tilted to one side.

"Are you with the hotel? Is everything all right?"

His tanned face was pinched with the cold, and he gripped my arm as I caught my breath, worn out from having trekked through the snow.

"I'm sorry to interrupt you, Mr. St. John. As far as I know, everyone is fine. I was wondering if I could ask you a few questions?"

A brief flash of annoyance flitted across his face before he settled his features into an amicable smile.

"Of course. Do you mind if we walk and talk? I need to keep moving."

Oh, I minded, particularly because he was pointing in the opposite direction of the warm buildings, but I would not pass up this chance.

"Absolutely. How are you holding up?"

He gave me an appraising look before focusing on the trail in front of us.

"I appreciate your concern, but I doubt you walked all this way to check on my mental health. Out with it, Miss Brooks, is it?"

I couldn't hide my startled expression as I realized he'd remembered my name. We'd met only in passing, during the welcome celebration, and we hadn't spoken since. His lips turned up, and he shook his head.

"I've heard your name from Sassy Jermain one or two times. I assume you're looking for information to help clear Marsburg? I can't blame you. He's a good man. I've known him for years and I know darn well he wouldn't kill Rebecca."

Again, he had me at an impasse. What I thought was going to be a difficult maneuver, requiring all my skills to worm out the information I wanted, was instead being handed to me on a platter. I turned my face towards his so he could see my smile.

"Well, you've made this task a lot easier, Mr. St. John. Can you tell me if you feel the same way about the rest of the ski team?"

His eyes sparkled as he chuffed a breath of surprise.

"I like your style, Ms. Brooks. Please, call me Chris. There's no need to be so formal. We have a shared goal of justice."

"Then, please call me Eden. You didn't answer my question, though."

He let out another exhalation and shook his head, giving me a rueful look before flashing his white teeth.

"You'd never think to look at you that you've the tenacity of a bulldog. Still, I can't say it's not appreciated. Is there a member of my team you're interested in? I'd answer you straight away, but I've been working out scenarios in my head, and I'm afraid they're muddled. That's why I'm out here running. It helps me think."

I thanked my lucky stars that I didn't require cold weather exercise to make my brain work.

"Well, there's Sassy, of course. I didn't miss the way she talked about Rebecca. I'm guessing the two weren't close?"

"You could say that. Did they hate one another? Not in my estimation. No, their relationship was merely competitive nearly always, switching to supportive when a championship was on the line. Don't mistake a competitive spirit for a murderous one. Sassy comes from a wonderful family. She's calculating, but not malicious. She'd weigh the odds before acting. No, I don't think she did it. Who's next?"

We worked through each of the team members before reaching the end of the woods and turning around. When I saw how far away the main lodge was, I nearly whimpered. I hadn't realized we'd come so far. A pang went through me as I realized how vulnerable I was out here with a man I didn't know. Had I put too much stock into the murderer being on the team while ignoring the coach? I didn't think so, but stranger things had happened. I shivered in my coat and forged ahead, hoping for the best.

"I saved Kendra for last," I said, puffing a little as we walked. "Given her history."

I hazarded a glance in his direction, watching his expression. I wasn't sure how much stock to put into what I'd read on the message board, but from his face, I saw immediately the report was true.

"Ah, I see you uncovered her unsavory past. Yes, Kendra has a history of getting what she wants, no matter what. You could say it was parents with too much money and too few boundaries, or an inborn desire to win at all costs."

"You'd want someone like that on your team?" I said, stopping in shock. "Someone who you know injured an innocent person just so they could get ahead?"

St. John shook his head slowly before shrugging.

"The desire to win comes in many forms. Is Kendra a good person? No, I don't believe she is. Is she an excellent skier? She has the potential to be a world-class athlete," he said, holding up a hand. "If, and it's a big if, that desire to win could be channeled in the right way. Her parents have a lot of money, a lot of pull, and zero boundaries for their baby girl. When she needed a new team, I couldn't say no."

We started walking again, and I jammed my hands further into my pockets as my mind spun. I noticed he wasn't saying something, but I wasn't sure if I was reading him right.

"Do you think she did it?"

He let out a breath, and I watched as it steamed in front of us before evaporating. He inhaled sharply through his nose, the sound loud in the still morning air.

"It's possible. I hesitate to point the finger at her, though. Could she hurt someone in a fit of anger? Maybe. But she is a shrewd creature who I've not known to lose her temper. Rebecca was strangled, which is typically an act of sudden violence, right? I don't know if she has that in her."

I'd gone through the entire team, unable to find a motive for most of them, which left me just one person who was there that night and had something to potentially lose.

"Do you think it was Ash?"

"Oh, Ashland. He's a wild card. I can't say with any certainty that he's the one, but I'll admit, I suspect him the most. In all fairness, that could be because I don't want it to be someone on my team. If it is, I've failed, not just as a coach, but as someone who's in charge of helping these athletes reach their potential."

He trailed off, his face cloudy. I was stuck trying to figure out what to say when he turned to me.

"Eden, if you have no further questions, I'd like to continue my run. Who knows, maybe something will occur to me along the way. If I think of anything helpful, I'll get in touch, okay?"

He didn't give me a chance to respond, turning to run back the way we'd just walked. Unless I wanted to run after him, which was a big no, I wasn't getting anything more from Christian St. John. I watched him for a moment before turning back towards the lodge.

"I thought he'd never leave. I've been trailing you forever."

I started at the sound of a soft voice coming from the trees.

"Who's there?"

"It's me, Willow."

The small tortoiseshell cat picked her way fastidiously through the snow, shaking her delicate paws with each step. She came to a stop, sat, and wrapped her tail tightly around her hindquarters. Her beautiful fur was fluffed up as far as it could go.

"Hi, Willow. You look cold. Is everything okay?"

"Oh, I'm fine. It's not too bad this morning. I scented you through the woods and I just had to catch you. I found him!"

Her little face was full of excitement as she looked up at me, eyes shining. It took me a second to realize what she was talking about.

"The other cat? You did?"

She nodded and pointed her muzzle back at the trees.

"He was right over there. I asked him to stay put. He's agreed to talk to you, but we'd better hurry. He didn't seem sure. Oh, I hope he didn't take off."

She leapt towards the woods, bypassing the drifts of snow, and I could hear her skittering through the brush. I hustled after her, wincing as a snow-laden branch smacked me in the face. I blundered on ahead, coming to a stop when I saw her waiting for me. Whiskers curved into a smile.

"I forgot you're so big you can't get through here like I can. We need to hurry, though."

I panted, hands on my knees, and nodded.

"Go ahead, I'll catch up. Is it far?"

"Not very," she said, leaping away.

I trailed after, making a mental note to take advantage of the gym facilities in the lodge more often. It was an employee perk, but I hadn't used it much. Finally, we came to a stop in front of a mottled tabby with long fur. His long nose led to a pair of pale yellow eyes which were full of fear.

He edged away, fur on end, when Willow sprang over to him, nosing him back into place.

"This is Eden, Dex. She won't hurt us."

He looked at me, eyes still wide, and moved his head up and down slightly.

"Willow says you can talk to us, but I don't think that's true. I only stayed to prove her wrong. I'd like to be on my way. I don't want to stay here too long."

"Hi, Dex. It's nice to meet you. I appreciate you staying so we could talk."

He gave a startled hop and looked at Willow, eyes goggling. She flipped her tail up in the air.

"I told you. Now, tell her what you saw. It's very important."

He shifted his position, wrapping his tail tightly around him. His powerful shoulders hunched, and he looked ready to spring away at any second.

"I was hunting near the back of that building over there," he said slowly, motioning with his head. "There's a good trash can back there where I can typically find food. Anyway, I heard voices, and turned to run, but something made me stop. There was a strange smell in the air. It reminded me of a place I used to live."

I cocked my head to the side, intrigued.

"What do you mean?"

His eyes took on a faraway look as he answered.

"There was a little girl who I used to see when I lived in town, near the park. She always brought me little treats. She's the one who called me Dex. I followed her home one day, you know, just to try it, but I didn't like her house. It smelled of anger. The big human there was always yelling. I liked the little girl, but I couldn't stay there. I tried to have her follow me, so she could leave that place, too, but she didn't understand," he said, trailing off, eyes full of sadness. "That's what I smelled a few nights ago. It was so familiar, it startled me, and I stopped."

My heart wrenched in my chest. Not only for Dex, but for the little girl in his story. I crouched down, not caring if my knees got wet in the snow.

"I'm sorry about that, Dex. What did you see?"

"I saw three humans, and they were arguing. I couldn't make out what they were saying, but I heard one of them make a terribly gurgling sound and I smelled death. I ran. I came back just to see what happened, but there were too many people around and the scent of death was much stronger. I headed for the woods, then."

I rocked back, startled. We'd been so sure it was one person.

"Wait, three people? Are you sure?"

He nodded, chest puffing up.

"I am. Two women and a man, from what I could tell. I'm sorry, that's all I know."

"Thank you, Dex. I'm sorry you had to go through that again. Did you say you lived in a town near here?" I asked, mind spinning.

"Yep. I've been on the move for a while, but it's not that far away. Why?"

"Do you think you'd know the house where that little girl lived?"

He gave me a wary look as he nodded slowly.

"I might. Why?"

"From your description, the girl was living in an abusive house. Maybe we could help her."

He took a small step in my direction, his eyes blazing with hope.

"You would do that? I wished I could help her. She was always so sad. But I'm just a cat."

I nodded and smiled at the big tom. Now that he was closer, I could spot the tiny scars on his face and ears. He'd had a rough life, but he cared about the fate of that little girl.

"If I can, I will. I know a local police officer. If you wouldn't mind going for a ride in my car, I can see if we can find that house."

He backed away, glancing at Willow.

"I don't know. How do I know if I can trust you?"

"Oh, I'll go with you," Willow said, hopping over to nose him again. "Don't be a fraidy-cat. I'll need to get permission from Fig, though. I can't run off and leave the clowder in a lurch."

He settled, shifting around a little in the snow.

"I'll do it. Just give me the word."

"I won't be able to go today," Willow said, sitting next to the big tabby. "We've got a huge hunting party planned, and we all need to help. Maybe tomorrow, though? It's up to Fig. Do you want to come, Dex?" she asked, dipping her head.

He shifted again, obviously uncomfortable.

"You know how I feel about lots of cats around. Maybe. I don't know. I'll be around."

He stalked off, tail held low, and melted into the trees. Willow watched him and heaved a sigh as she looked at me.

"He's not cut out for clowder life, is he?"

I knew little about what the requirements for clowder life were, but it was obvious he was a loner cat. A loner cat who worried about a little girl. Plans started swirling in my mind as I focused back on Willow.

"I don't think so. Maybe that's not his place, though. He might have another calling."

Understanding dawned in her eyes and she dipped her head towards me.

"I'll check with Fig. Are you going to come with Luke tonight to the feeding point?"

"I hope so. If not, I'll come out here tomorrow, okay? Stay warm, Willow. Does the clowder need anything?"

"We're fine," she said, flipping her tail.

"Good hunting," I said, as she sprang away, racing through the trees again.

I got back on my feet and started through the woods in the opposite direction, at a much slower pace. Three people, he'd said. I hadn't even considered that more than one person was involved in Rebecca's death. This put an entirely new spin on her murder. I ran through dozens of scenarios on my way back to the lodge, each one increasingly bizarre, before shaking my head in doubt. How were we going to figure this out?

Chapter Fifteen

C onsidering how my morning started, the rest of the day went relatively smoothly. Was I able to focus on any work tasks? No, I wasn't. I tried, but my brain was too preoccupied with listing out facts and coming up empty when I needed answers. I was ready to get out of my head once dinner time rolled around. I closed the course I'd pulled up on my computer, and hadn't even looked at it, and turned off my lights.

I walked into the lobby on autopilot, fiddling with my bag as I walked around the front desk and ran smack into someone who definitely shouldn't have been there. My head snapped back as I looked into a pair of familiar eyes.

"Ethan? What are you doing here?"

Wendy flashed me a guilty look as she slid what looked like a cabin keycard across the desk. Ethan slipped it into his pocket and smiled.

"Checking in. It looks like the cabin next to yours is open, which is great. I appreciate Marsburg making this happen."

My mouth opened and closed until I felt like a fish. Wendy covered her mouth to hide what looked suspiciously like a laugh before she got control of herself.

"Eden, isn't it wonderful that Detective Rhodes cares enough about our safety to stay here and make sure nothing happens to us? After what was found in your door, I'd think you'd be grateful for his protection."

I narrowed my eyes at Wendy, promising later retribution.

"Yes, wonderful. That's just the word I'd use for it."

"I'm glad we're all in agreement," Ethan said, his eyes twinkling. "I'll just toss my bag into my cabin. Wendy was just saying I was welcome to eat dinner with everyone in the dining hall. What number did you say I was in, Wendy?"

"Nine. Right between Charlie and Eden," she said, wincing in my direction.

"Perfect. Thanks again."

He tapped the desk before sweeping his arm out towards the door. I shot Wendy one more glare before trudging to the door. A different patrol car was now in the lot. It was a good thing we were all law-abiding citizens, or we'd feel cramped by the very obvious police presence.

"So, Wendy was saying the meals here are fantastic," Ethan said, breaking the silence that fell between us as we walked through the snow.

"Yeah, it's great. I think tonight is roast beef night, so you're in luck."

At least one of us was. I appreciated the lengths he was going to keep us safe, myself in particular, but I couldn't help but feel awkward. We had the strangest relationship, and I wasn't sure living in proximity was going to make it any better.

"I love roast beef."

We came to a stop, and I pointed at the cabin.

"This is you. I think I'll just stay in tonight," I said, right before remembering my fridge was empty.

"Eden," he said, putting his hands on his hips. "Don't do that. I know this is a strange situation, but I need to be here. It's obvious we're dealing with someone very dangerous and you, and everyone here, are at risk. Besides, I'd appreciate it if you'd go with me and smooth over the introductions. Not everyone is going to be happy I'm here."

Guilt smacked me right in the face as I looked into his eyes. Typically, he was well-assured, without being overconfident. Now? He looked almost tentative as his eyes searched my face. Why was I being so prickly? He was here to do his job, and I was rude. I forced a smile and nodded.

"Of course, I'd be happy to do that," I said, rubbing my forehead. "I'm sorry. I'm out of sorts. This has been a lot."

"I know it has. I'll just toss my bag inside. I can unpack later."

"I need to check on Jasper. I'll be right out."

I walked the short distance to my cabin and found Jasper cuddled up in my chair, his head on my scarf. A genuine smile spread across my face as he yawned and tossed an arm forward.

"Yeah, big stretch," I said, closing the door behind me. "We've got a neighbor tonight, bud, so we'll want to keep our voices down."

He scented the air before he hopped down and stretched.

"Detective Rhodes is staying next door. That's good."

"You can smell that? Dear Lord, I hope you don't think I reek," I said, sniffing my armpit on the sly. "If you can smell him through two layers of walls, what must it be like living in here with me?"

"Relax, you smell lovely," he said, giving me a kitty eye roll. "What's for supper tonight?"

"Roast beef with a side of awkwardness," I said, under my breath. "But I think you've got the choice of chicken or turkey."

I walked over to the kitchenette and pulled out two food packets. He cocked his head to the side before nodding decisively.

"Turkey. I like that stuff."

I got his meal sorted, refreshed his water bowl before leaning against the counter. There was so much I wanted to say, but it would have to wait for later.

"I'll check in on the clowder tonight after dinner. Any messages?"

He stopped eating for a second and looked over at me.

"Just let them know they're in my thoughts."

"Will do. They had a hunting party today, so I'm not sure how hungry everyone will be."

A look of longing shot over Jasper's face as he looked out the window.

"Those are the best days," he whispered. "Everyone working together to feed the clowder. I will miss that."

"Hey, maybe we can take part. I mean, I can't, but next time maybe we can arrange for you to visit during a hunt?"

He considered it for a second before turning back to his bowl.

"We'll see."

A soft knock on my door made my shoulders fill with tension.

"That's Ethan. I've got to go, but I'll be back in a little while. I'll bring you some treats."

He flicked his tail in my direction as I walked towards the door. Ethan was waiting on the other side, looking up and down the row of cabins.

"Hey, sorry. I wanted to make sure he was fed before I ate."

"No rush," Ethan said. "Who lives in that cabin?"

I looked to where he was pointing and smiled.

"That's Danny's. He's probably already at the dining hall. He's not one to miss a meal."

He filled the short walk to the hall with questions about the other cabin inhabitants and by the time we walked in, I was feeling easier about his closeness. I led him over to the buffet and handed him a tray.

"Help yourself to whatever looks good. Ooh, I see mashed potatoes," I said, looking down the line. "Those are the best. I can't believe Danny and Charlie left some behind."

I filled up my plate and walked down the row until I spotted Luke. He looked tired, but still smiled at me.

"Hey, Eden. Want to come with me to feed the cats tonight?"

"Absolutely," I said, smiling back. "Oh Luke, this is Ethan Rhodes. He's staying with us during his investigation."

Ethan's shoulder brushed mine as he reached across the buffet to shake Luke's hand.

"Nice to meet you. What's this about cats?"

"Oh, Eden and I usually feed the local clowder the leftovers every night. It's been so nice having her help."

"Great. Mind if I tag along tonight?"

I minded. I minded a lot. It was hard enough to talk to the cats when Luke was around, but he was used to my chatter and never seemed to listen too closely. I needed to talk to Willow tonight to see when she could get away on our special mission with Dex.

"Not at all," Luke said, oblivious to the silent message I was beaming at him. "The more the merrier."

Great. Just great. Ethan grinned and nudged me with an elbow.

"I'm guessing that's Danny?"

I looked over at our usual table where Charlie, Danny, and Josh were already seated and nodded. Danny was waving at me while Charlie's eyes were as big as the plates on the table.

"Yep, that's him. Come on, let's sit."

We put our trays on the table and Danny hopped up to grab an extra chair for Ethan, while shooting me what he must have thought were covert looks, but unfortunately, fell a little short.

"I suppose you're wondering why I'm here," Ethan said as he took a seat. "I've met most of you before, but I'm Detective Rhodes. I'll be staying in a cabin here for a few days."

"We appreciate the police department looking out for us," Danny said, his voice a little loud. "We're all law-abiding citizens here and there's no need to worry about us."

Charlie rolled her eyes and stabbed her fork in his direction.

"Knock it off, Danny. You're laying it on a little thick. Hi, Detective Rhodes. It's nice to see you again."

Somehow, we got through the meal with a minimum of embarrassment. Charlie looked tired and kept yawning. I leaned closer to her.

"Are you okay?"

"Yeah, my sleep schedule is all shot. If this keeps up, I may have to switch with Wendy and go back to working days," she said, shuddering. "Except I hate days."

"You'll be fine," I said, patting her arm. "Maybe try staying up a little longer than you usually do and you'll reset."

"A girl can hope," she said, flinging a glance at Ethan. "Are you okay?"

"I guess so," I said, folding my napkin. "I've got a lot to report, but now isn't a good time. I'll text you later."

She tapped her finger to the side of her nose before noticing Ethan had become very interested in our conversation. She smiled awkwardly at him before leaping to her feet and giving Danny a pointed look.

"I've gotta go so Wendy can eat. See you later, everyone."

Danny shoved half a dinner roll in his mouth and jumped up.

"I'll come with you, Charlie. Hey, hold up."

Josh chuckled as he stood and grabbed the trays they'd left behind.

"Eden, you want me to grab yours too? And yours, Detective Rhodes?"

"Thanks, Josh," I said. "That's nice of you."

"Meh, I'm headed that way, anyway. Stay safe, Eden," he said. "I've asked Danny to make sure Charlie gets to the lodge safely. We can't be too careful right now."

He headed out, leaving us alone at our now empty table. I glanced at the clock and stood.

"I usually meet Luke out back and help him carry the trays. Are you sure you want to come? It's pretty cold tonight."

"Absolutely. I love cats. I'm curious to see more of this clowder."

Blast it. Well, I tried. He followed me outside and we waited for Luke, the ease of our prior conversation lost. I nudged the snow around with my toe until the doors finally opened and Luke popped out.

"Hi, Detective, Eden. The cats are going to be so happy tonight. They love this gravy."

He talked all the way to the treeline, carrying the food and the conversation. We got to our usual spot where we fed the cats and I jogged ahead to clear off the platters from their covering of snow.

"It's so quiet out here," Ethan said, turning slowly in a circle. "What a beautiful night."

He was right. The night, although frigid, had its beauty. The stars were brilliant in the clear sky and the moon was just coming up over the trees. It was almost magical in its stillness.

Soon, I could just make out the sound of tiny feet in the snow as the cats arrived. One by one, they entered the clearing, lining up. Ethan was silent as he watched Fig stride towards us. She came to a stop in front of him, scenting the air.

"Why is he here?" she asked, staring at me with her blazing yellow eyes.

I couldn't reply outright, so I got creative.

"Thanks again for helping us tonight, Ethan. These are the cats."

She seemed to understand and tilted her head to the side, considering Ethan for a long moment before stepping back.

"He'll do. Cats, let's eat."

Ethan stood with us as we watched the cats go through their normal pattern of eating. The younger cats were shy of him and I knelt, pulling on his arm so he'd do the same. He sank to the ground and watched in wonder as the smaller cats began eating.

"They're so organized," he said, his voice soft.

"They are," Luke said, nodding. "I like to use this time to look them over and make sure everyone's okay. Eden is the one who truly has won their trust, though. They love her."

Ethan looked at me, his eyes full of an emotion I couldn't quite name, and he nodded slowly.

"I can see why."

I spotted Willow, and she flared her eyes at me, looking between Luke, Ethan, and me. I shook my head slightly. I needed to know if Fig had given permission, but now wasn't the time to ask. I kept eye contact and hoped she'd understand. Somehow, I'd have to get back out here so we could talk.

Before too long, the last cat had eaten its fill and Fig took her portion, holding it in her mouth to eat later. She swept her tail, and like magic, all the cats melted back into the trees, leaving us once again in stillness.

"That was incredible," Ethan said. "Thank you for letting me experience this. I'd like to come tomorrow night, if you don't mind."

I couldn't turn him down, especially considering the look on his face. He'd been charmed by the cats and a part of my heart cheered. If there was ever to be... well, I wouldn't think about that. Not now. I stood as Luke stacked the trays he'd brought.

"It's really cool," Luke said. "They're so interesting. Oh, Eden, how's Jasper? He looked so excited when you brought him out here the other day."

"He's doing a lot better," I said, ignoring Ethan's questioning look. "He was pretty happy to see his old buddies, though."

We walked back to the resort, and I let Luke carry the conversation again. I looked back over my shoulder at the trees, giving Willow a silent promise that I'd talk to her, and soon. Dex needed our help, and so did a little girl in town. Before I knew it, I was standing in front of my cabin with Ethan.

"I had a wonderful night," he said, leaning against the door frame. "Thanks for that."

"You don't need to thank me," I said, looking down.

"Yes. I do. Eden, I know things have been a little, um... Well, oh shoot, I don't know how to say it."

He took off his stocking hat and scratched at the back of his head. His bangs fell over his forehead and I had to physically restrain myself from smoothing them back. Our eyes met, and I swallowed hard. I wasn't ready for this.

"Thanks for coming to feed the cats," I said, putting my hand on the doorknob. "I'll see you tomorrow?"

He got the message and took a step back, straightening.

"Definitely. I'll be on watch, but please stay safe. If you need to leave your cabin, let me know. I'll be happy to escort you anywhere."

Well, there went my idea of going back to talk to Willow tonight. I said a silent prayer and nodded at Ethan.

"Okay. Good night."

"Good night, Eden."

I walked inside and closed the door firmly, leaning against it. So many thoughts and emotions swirled through my mind that it was almost overwhelming. I took a deep breath, flipped on the light and smiled at Jasper as he walked towards me, tail held high. A night cuddling with my cat was definitely what I needed right now. Tomorrow, with all of its questions and worries, could wait. At least for a few hours.

Chapter Sixteen

W hether I subconsciously slept better, knowing Ethan was next door, or the events of the past few days finally caught up with me, I ended up sleeping in and completely ignoring my alarm. Jasper watched, amusement clear on his face, as I scampered around my room, throwing on clothes and trying to re-braid my hair all at the same time.

"You've been early every day this week," he said, settling his head between his paws. "A few minutes late isn't a big deal, is it?"

"I never like to be late for work," I said, around the hair tie I was holding in my teeth. "I wanted to talk to Willow this morning, too, and now that won't be possible. Argh!"

I keeled over onto the bed as I tried to put a boot on with one hand. Jasper shook his head and got up, stretching.

"Wouldn't all of this be easier if you did one thing at a time? All I can say is it's a good thing I'm a cat. We're never late or early. We arrive precisely..."

"When you mean to," I said, finishing the quote with a snort. We'd recently read *The Fellowship of the Ring* together and he'd loved it. "Like a wizard. I know it's silly, Jasper, but I've always prided myself on my punctuality."

"There are worse things to worry about. Now, if you don't mind, I think it's time for me to get back to my nap."

He gave me a head bump before curling up right by my pillow. I watched him for a second before my anxiety ratcheted up a notch and I finished getting ready, albeit at a slightly less frenetic pace. I placed a kiss on his little forehead before heading outside, still half in and half out of my coat.

Ethan's door was open as I dashed past, hoping he wouldn't want to chat. His shout brought me to a stop.

"Eden?"

"Sorry I'm late for work," I said, waving and continuing on. "I'll talk with you later."

I wanted to look back to see if he was watching me. It sure felt like he was, but I resisted the urge and kept plowing through the snow. I'd missed the shift change, and breakfast, which meant Charlie was probably already tucked into bed and Wendy would be at the front desk.

As I walked inside, I came to a stop when I saw the people standing at the desk. Rob and his family were there, their faces drawn, and Wendy looked overwhelmed. I hurriedly shucked off my coat and joined her behind the desk.

"Oh, thank goodness, you're here," she said in an undertone. "I don't know what to do. They're here to collect Rebecca's things. Do you think that's okay? I can't find Mr. Marsburg to ask."

"Is there a problem?"

The change in Diane Yardley was astonishing. During the banquet, she'd been so poised, gleaming like a silver goddess with her white hair. Now, she looked like she'd aged twenty years in just a few days. My heart wrenched as I noticed Mr. Yardley looked just as drawn. Rob was staring out the windows, his shoulders hunched. He'd been so full of energy when we'd first met, and it looked like all the life had been sucked out of him.

"No, not at all. We just need to check something. It won't take a minute."

I dug in my pocket for my phone to call Ethan to ensure the

room had been cleared, but apparently, he'd been right on my heels. He walked through the door and spotted the Yardleys.

"Mr. and Mrs. Yardley," he said, pausing in the entryway.

"Detective Rhodes," Robert Yardley said, his tone as icy as the walkways outside. "We're here for our daughter's things. I assume that won't be a problem?"

"Not at all," Ethan said, glancing at us. "In fact, I'll be happy to escort you up to the room. We had to log a few things as potential evidence, but once this is over, you'll be able to pick them up at the station."

"Have you found out who murdered my sister yet?" Rob asked, his eyes visibly reddened as he turned to face us.

Ethan shook his head and stuck his hands in his pockets. "We're still working on it."

"Well, work harder, dammit," Diane said, her voice cracking. "My little girl is dead and we demand justice. I don't see what's taking so long. You know very well who is responsible."

"Now, Di," Robert said, taking his wife's arm. "You understand it takes time to build an airtight case. The detective has to be sure all of his ducks are in a row, so whoever did it doesn't get off on a technicality. I like it as little as you, but we know how the justice system works."

"Mom, it wasn't James. We've gone over this. He loved Rebecca dearly, and they talked constantly. He had no reason to kill her," Rob said, his hand shaking as he rubbed his face and turned to Ethan. "I need to get a few things out of my room as well."

Wendy slid the key cards across the desk and Diane snagged them without a word. Ethan shot me a look as he went with them towards the elevator. I bit my lip as I waited for the door to slide shut, blocking them from our view. Wendy let out an enormous sigh.

"Gosh, I feel so badly for that family. I wish there was something we could do. Has Ethan said anything about who he suspects?"

"No. I've shared everything we've learned, but he hasn't reciprocated. I don't think he can. At least Rob doesn't think it was our boss. I just wish we knew who it was. Knowing they're out there makes me so nervous."

I crossed my arms and rubbed them as I nodded in agreement. Footsteps banged down the stairs and two members of the ski team came into view. Troy's face split into a huge smile as he spotted me and I shrank back without meaning to.

"There she is. I haven't seen you in a while," he said, leaning against the desk, beaming. "I missed your face."

How was I supposed to answer that? Luckily, Kendra jumped in and saved me.

"What does that even mean? That's got to be one of the weirdest sayings I've ever heard. Don't you just miss a person? Why their face?"

Troy's eyes flashed as he looked at Kendra, before clearing as he turned back to me.

"Would you mind showing us the gym? I know the coach likes to go for runs, but that's not really my thing," he said, curling up his arm. "I need to pump some iron to keep these guns in tip-top shape."

Gag. I turned to Wendy, desperate for rescue, but the blasted phone rang at the exact wrong time. She answered it with a grimace. I guess that meant I had little choice. It looked like I was going to suffer Troy's presence for just a little longer. I pasted on a smile I didn't feel and nodded sharply.

"Sure. If you'll follow me, it's right this way."

I walked as quickly as I could, but of course, the ski team members were way taller than and their strides devoured the distance I tried to put between us.

"Hey, what's the hurry? Your hair is seriously dope. Have I told you that?"

He reached over to grab my braid, wrapping the end around his hand. I wanted to rip my hair out of his hand and scream at him to leave me alone, but I knew I couldn't do that.

"The gym is typically open until ten at night," I said, falling back on formality as I wrenched my neck to the side to free my braid. "It opens up at nine, but we try to have it ready before then."

"Cool," Kendra said, looking around the hallway as I race-walked them towards the gym. "This place is kinda cool. It's super dated, though."

"Oh look at you, acting like you know anything about decor," Troy said, rolling his eyes. "Don't pay any attention to her. I never do."

We made it to the door, and I used my hotel keycard to open it for them and stepped back.

"Here you go. Everything is pretty self explanatory. There's a hotel phone if you need anything, though. Wendy will help you."

"Hey, what's the hurry?" Troy said, leaning over me to place his hand on the wall behind me. "I wouldn't mind a tour of your facilities."

I swallowed hard and ducked under his arm, desperate to get out of here. I should've felt safe with another woman present, but strangely, I didn't. I noticed Kendra shut the door and leaned against it, a strange look on her face as she crossed her arms over her chest.

"If you'll excuse me, I need to get back to work."

I tried to push past her.

"Yeah, that's not happening," she said, drawling her words as her eyes searched the corners of the ceiling. "We need to talk. I told you there weren't any cameras in here, Troy. It's the perfect spot."

Icy fingers of dread went down my spine as she stared through my soul with her expressionless eyes. What had I gotten myself into? I stepped back and bumped into Troy, who fastened his arms around mine, holding me tight.

"No need to rush off, little one," he said, leaning so close I could feel his breath on my neck. "Like Kendra said, we just want to talk."

The sauna beeped, startling everyone, and Troy whipped his head in that direction, dragging me to stand in front of him.

"What was that? Is someone in here?"

"It was the sauna, coming to temp. We turn it on every morning when we open the gym."

I tried to see through the door. Was someone in there? It wasn't a big sauna, and the glass door let you look right inside. From where

I was standing, it looked empty. Troy looked over my shoulder at it and then his hold on me relaxed just a little.

"That seems like a waste of electricity," he said, making a tsking sound. "Haven't you heard about going green?"

His grip continued to slacken, and I stepped forward as fast as I could, hoping to break free, but he only grabbed me even tighter and made that sound again.

"Now don't do that. It would be a shame if something happened to you, wouldn't it? Especially since there are so many dangerous things in this gym. I mean, it would be terrible if you slipped and this barbell just fell on top of your head. Gyms can be so dangerous, can't they?"

"Wendy knows you brought me back here. Whatever you're planning, it won't."

"Oh, really?" Kendra asked in a sing-song voice. "Even if we rush back to the front desk, full of fear at the accident we just witnessed?"

She arranged her face into a horrified expression as Troy laughed.

"Yeah, that's right, babe. Just like that. Now, do the voice."

Kendra's face momentarily reshaped into a wicked grin before going back to her mock expression and speaking in a breathy voice.

"It was awful. I've seen nothing like it. We just wanted to see the equipment in the gym and the poor girl slipped in a puddle of water and went down, hitting her head on the way. We came for help right away. Oh please, hurry!"

Troy drew me back towards his body and I stumbled on his foot, looking down at his boots. Boots I recognized. They'd been the same ones I'd fallen over in Kendra's room, right before the ski team showed up. Dread filled my chest as I put the last piece into place.

"It was you. Both of you. You killed Rebecca."

The grip on my arms intensified, and I cried out, even though I knew it was useless. The gym was tucked away. Unless someone passed by, no one was going to hear me. They'd picked their spot well. My only chance of escape was being blocked by Kendra, and from the strength I felt in Troy's grip, breaking free wasn't an option. My heart sank as I realized just how much danger I was in.

Chapter Seventeen

The hotel phone was just a few steps away, but it might as well have been miles thanks to the pickle I was in. I glanced at it and tried to shift my body in that direction. If I could just knock it down and press one button, Wendy would send help. Troy seemed to sense what I was doing and yanked me in the other direction. I raised my chin, unwilling to give up. Jasper needed me, and I wouldn't go without a fight.

"Aren't you just making this worse for yourselves?" I asked, gritting my teeth from the pain in my shoulders. "You've already killed once. You're just going to get harsher sentences for doing it again."

"Like we're gonna get caught," Kendra scoffed, studying a nail. "Shoot, I broke another one. Does this rinky-dink resort even have an on-staff manicurist? Probably not, huh?"

Fury shot through my chest as I watched this self-absorbed woman who had literally no respect for life.

"Eventually you will. You might get away today, but you can't run forever. You can't just kill people and get away with it."

"See, that's where we're different from people like you," Troy said, pulling me tight against his chest. "We've got powerful families who want to see us succeed. That's what really matters. Besides, I've been thinking, Kendra. Why go to the trouble of reporting this one dead? We can go back to our rooms, making sure of course to be seen, get our gym gear, and when we come back, we can find her body and something that will tie Marsburg to her death. I'm a genius."

I refused to let despair win, but it was getting harder. Now they were going to frame Marsburg?

"How are you gonna do that?" Kendra asked, cocking her head to the side. "I mean, I love the idea. It's definitely a winner, but it seems complicated."

"Just leave it to me, babe. I've got this."

Could this man be any cockier? Dislike finally dampened my fear so I could think straight. Wendy knew I'd gone with them and she knew where we were going. If I could keep them talking, she'd realize I'd been gone for too long and she'd send help. Besides, Ethan was just a few floors away. I just needed to buy myself some time.

"Why did you kill Rebecca? Aren't your families all friends or something?"

Troy laughed, sending vibrations down my back as he pulled me up against his chest again.

"Friends, that's a good one. More like they were the ones who were always in the spotlight and we had to play second fiddle while they got all the accolades. Do you know how infuriating it is to be second best to people when you're the one with all the talent? It's been that way since we were on the bunny hills together. Rob's folks always had more money, more power, more prestige. Do you think he was team captain because he was a better skier than me? No, it's because the Yardleys paid for all our trips, all of our gear."

I struggled to find the reason that meant Rebecca had to die. None of this made sense. Kendra rolled her eyes and smirked at Rob.

"She still doesn't get it. I can tell from her stupid face. Rebecca was going to get married and retire. This was supposed to be her last event, and I'd finally be able to take her place. And then good old Rob had to find Ash in bed with Chrissy, and of course, he ran to tell his little sister. She was going to go at least for another year, maybe two. Do you have any idea how damaging that would be for my career? Every year I'm not at the top means another year of talent down the drain. She was getting slow. I'm way faster, but my last name isn't Yardley, so it didn't matter."

"Couldn't you just join another team? I mean, murder seems a little extreme."

Her eyes narrowed, and she walked closer to me, stabbing at my chest with one of her pointed nails.

"Do you know how hard it is to get on a ski team?"

"Especially with your rep, Kendra," Troy snickered. "Talk about a dumb move. If you'd waited for another event, that girl probably would've blown out her knee anyway, and no one would've known it was you. Amateur. Rebecca was on to you. That's why she blabbed to St. John and made it so you couldn't travel with the team. You need to learn the art of subtlety, babe."

"Whatever," she said, rolling her eyes as she went back to lean on the door. "Can we wrap this up? I've got other stuff I need to do today."

I tried to twist around so I could see Troy's face, but he held me fast as I squirmed. From the strength in his hands, I assumed he was the one to strangle Rebecca, but I still didn't understand what he had to gain. Where was everyone? Surely Wendy had to have noticed I'd been gone too long. Sweat ran down my spine and I shivered.

"I can see what you had to gain, Kendra, but I don't understand you, Troy," I said, hoping to buy a little more time. "Why did you strangle Rebecca?"

"Kendra and I were talking, and I saw the opportunity to get two birds with one stone. Rob's been captain for too long. I'm usually at least five ticks faster on the downhill, but much like Kendra, I've got to wait in the wings so he can shine. I'm sick of it. I figured if we took out Rebecca, Rob would be too distraught to compete at the event and I'd finally get my chance. It was a win."

"And now the team isn't even going to compete. I've tried to get St. John to see the sense of going ahead in Rebecca's memory, but he's against it. I didn't even get that ring, either. This whole thing has just been one giant bummer," Kendra said, heaving a sigh. "If only Hallie hadn't come outside to smoke, I would've had it."

"You're the one who took the ring off her finger?" I asked, flabbergasted. "Why?"

"She had two engagement rings. Two! Who needs two of them? When I heard the doors open, I panicked and dropped it in the snow."

"We'll get rings, babe," Troy said. "Once we get back on the circuit and start winning some events, we'll have everything we want."

"You honestly can't believe you're going to get away with this," I said, squirming harder. "Someone is going to figure it out."

"That's where you're wrong, little one," Troy said, leaning so close I could smell his coffee breath. "I'm the one who has it all figured out. I just need to grab a few things and we're in the clear."

He released one of my shoulders and I tried to spin to make a break for it, but pulled up short when he grabbed my braid and wrapped it around his hand.

"Let me go!"

"No, I don't think I will," he said, wrapping the braid even tighter. "Huh, it's all real. I thought for sure you had extensions. How long did it take you to grow this?"

"Oh my God, stop talking about her hair and finish her."

He spun me around so I could see his face, and I recoiled once I saw his eyes. Whatever lived inside of Troy Lawton wasn't human. He was a monster with dead eyes. He let my braid go and the corner of his mouth quirked up.

"I wonder if I could strangle you with this?" he asked, waving the end of my braid in my face before he began wrapping it around my neck. "Only one way to find out."

"You're weird," Kendra said, her tone bland. "But if it gets the job done, I guess. Hurry! I still don't know how you plan to frame Marsburg."

I clawed at Troy's chest as he pulled at the end of my hair, cutting off my airway. My knees gave out, and the room darkened.

This was it. I was going to die in a hotel gym, strangled by my own hair. That thought gave me a burst of energy, and I scrabbled at Troy's hands, trying to loosen them. His evil smile filled my vision as it faded.

"Stop!"

A loud bang as the door shot open echoed through the room, and Troy released me suddenly. I fell to my knees, gasping, and tried to make sense of what was going on as precious air flooded back into my lungs.

"Put your hands up, both of you."

Tears ran down my face as I recognized Ethan's voice, and for a second, I was certain I was dreaming. Troy and Kendra were both on their knees, their eyes huge, as Ethan trained his service weapon on them. I looked towards the hall and realized it was full of uniformed police.

"There's been a misunderstanding, officer," Troy said, his voice set to full smarm. "We were only joking around."

"Yeah, we weren't going to actually hurt her. We just wanted to scare her," Kendra chimed in.

I jumped as the door to the sauna opened and a very red Alicia stepped out, sweat pouring off her face.

"That's not true. I heard everything, and I recorded it on my phone," she said, pointing towards the sauna. "I hid in the sauna's corner when I heard them come in, and I texted the police line once I heard what they were saying. Eden, I wouldn't have let them kill you. I just didn't know what to do."

My mind still hadn't caught up with the fact that I was still alive, even though the uniformed officers were cuffing Kendra and Troy and leading them out the room. Ethan turned to me, his heart in his eyes, and closed the distance between us in record time.

His hand trembled slightly as he carefully unwound the rest of my braid from my neck and helped me stand. What I saw in his eyes made my knees weak, and my mouth feel like the desert.

"Eden... Are you okay? Do you need to see the paramedics?"

I wasn't sure if hugging a police detective who'd just saved your life was professional, but I didn't care. I flung my arms around him and buried my face in his neck. He squeezed me back, hard.

"Thank you for coming. I didn't know..."

I glanced over Ethan's shoulder and saw Alicia was still alarmingly red. I stepped back and pulled myself together.

"Alicia, let's get you some water. You like you're going to pass out."

I hustled over to the corner where we kept the water dispenser and grabbed one of the tiny cups, looking at in disbelief. Alicia barked out a short laugh and pointed towards the lockers on the side of the room as she bent over.

"I've got my bottle in the locker there. 2-1-2. It's not locked."

Ethan got there just before I did, our hands brushing as we both reached for the clasp. A tiny jolt sparked through my hand, but I didn't think it was static electricity. No, this was something else entirely. I pulled my hand back and let him open the locker. Once I had Alicia's bottle in hand, I was too happy to retreat to the water cooler in confusion.

It slowly glugged out water as Ethan helped Alicia over to the bench on the other side of the room. Once the bottle was full, I joined them, sitting heavily next to her, head still reeling from the past half hour.

"You texted the police?" I asked once she'd taken a big drink.

Alicia leaned back and let out a gusty sigh as she nodded.

"I didn't want to risk calling. I'm grateful it works here. I was used to it in Aurora, where I grew up, but I wasn't sure it would work out here."

"We upgraded the system last year," Ethan said, hands on hips. "Dispatch passed it along to me since they knew I was out here already and sent the calvary. It's a good thing they did."

I nodded slowly, staring at my hands on my knees. Everything felt a little surreal, a little off. Minutes ago, I'd been certain I was done for. Now, I was sitting next to the person who was going to help me put away two monsters, and a man I definitely held feelings for. Feelings I didn't know what to do with.

Our eyes met over Alicia's head and he smiled, the corners of his eyes crinkling. Luckily, there was plenty to focus on. She took another huge drink of water and turned to Ethan.

"I'm ready to make my statement. I know how this all works. I remember when someone got shot in my apartment building when I was ten. I assume not much has changed."

I blinked, startled at her frank tone. I couldn't imagine what she'd seen on her way to becoming a world-class skier, and now, her future was completely up in the air, thanks to two people who'd taken their rivalries way too far.

"That's right, Alicia. I'll need to get statements from both of you. Eden, if you'd like to wait a little longer, I understand. Are you sure both of you don't need to see the paramedics? They're waiting in the parking lot."

I shook my head and stared at my hands again. My throat felt raw, but that could wait. I wouldn't risk forgetting one thing that would ensure Kendra and Troy stayed behind bars for the rest of their lives.

"I'm fine. I'm ready whenever you are."

"Me, too. I just got a little warm. I'll rehydrate while I talk. Eden, do you mind if I go first?"

I shook my head as I grabbed her water bottle to fill it. A familiar voice began shouting in the hall, and I turned to see Charlie, fighting to get through the crowd of officers.

"Eden! Oh my God, I swear if you're dead I'm going to kill you again," she said as soon as she saw me.

"I'm not dead," I said, holding up my hand while I delivered the water to Alicia. "But I would've been if it weren't for these two."

"I want to hear everything," she said, taking my shoulders while her eyes searched my face.

I shushed her and pulled her down to sit next to me while Alicia talked. Charlie gasped and took my hand as Alicia relayed what she'd heard.

Sooner than I'd liked, it was my turn. Charlie was right there, supporting me, as I walked back through everything. My other hand crept up to my throat as I remembered that horrible sensation of not being able to breathe. I trailed off, finally finished with my statement. Charlie looked at my braid and nodded decisively.

"That's it, we're cutting your hair. I'll do it myself. There is no way we're ever risking that happening again."

She looked serious, but something in her tone made me giggle. It started in fits and starts and before I knew it, I was laughing so hard tears came out of my eyes. Ethan stood as the men in the hallway peered in, likely wondering what on earth was wrong with me. I finally got myself under control, but it was a struggle.

"She needs some sugar. It's been quite a shock. I'd recommend some orange juice and something to eat. I have everything I need to prove murder and attempted murder. Eden, I'll be back later, okay? I'm just a call away if you need anything."

Alicia stood and patted my shoulder.

"I'm glad you didn't die. I wish I'd been more brave, but I..."

"Nonsense," I said, wiping my eyes. "You were plenty brave. Thanks to you, they're going away for a long time."

She chewed on her lip and looked towards the door, her expression conflicted.

"You'd think that, but I wouldn't count on it. The Lawtons and the Baldwins have plenty of pull. But my recording should help."

"You should get something to eat, too," I said, standing to embrace her. "You're still super pale."

She nodded, cheeks flushing.

"Thanks, Eden. I'll do that."

Alicia walked out of the gym and I watched as the hallway slowly cleared of people. Charlie cracked her gum loudly, startling me.

"Well, you heard the man. We need food, stat. I'm sure Luke and Iris will have something. Let's go."

She pulled me to my feet, and I followed her out of the gym, looking at the spot where I'd nearly breathed my last. I shook my head slowly, heart full of sorrow at Rebecca's death, and the future those two had thrown away. Thanks to Ethan and Alicia, I had a chance of finding my future. I wouldn't waste it.

Chapter Eighteen

Two months ago, the thought of chauffeuring three cats around town would have seemed improbable, if not impossible. But here we were, cruising around Valewood while Dex tried to get his bearings. Jasper rode shotgun, and I smiled as I realized how far he'd come since our last trip to town. The older cat was filling out, and he no longer seemed so frail. Willow's eyes were wide as she looked at the bustling little community.

"Do you remember the color of the house?" I asked, finally hitting on a way to narrow down our options.

Dex shifted in the backseat, meeting my eyes in the rearview mirror.

"I don't know how to describe it. It's so different sitting up this high. It changes my perspective completely."

I pulled to the side of the road and turned off the engine. We'd driven through all the neighborhoods twice, and Dex was looking a little frayed around the edges. Convincing him to get into a moving vehicle had been a challenge. If it hadn't been for Jasper volunteering to go, we wouldn't have made it this far. It was obvious Dex looked up to the former clowder leader and trusted him completely.

I couldn't fault Dex for his hesitation. His experience with humans so far hadn't been great, minus the little girl he'd become so fond of. He stared out the window, eyes wide. Willow leaned closer to him, brushing him with the tip of her tail.

"Do you remember the park where you used to meet the girl? Maybe we can retrace your steps?"

"Willow, you're a genius," I said as I pulled my phone out of my bag. "There can't be that many parks in Valewood. Let's see what we can find."

Jasper leaned closer, peering at my phone as I opened my map. He shook his head as I enlarged the view.

"We're that blue dot? How does it know where we are?"

"GPS," I said, focusing on the satellite view. "It looks like there are two parks. The first one is just two blocks that way. Let's try that one first."

Hope flared in Dex's wary eyes as I turned the car back on and we cruised forward. Improbable or not, I was enjoying spending my Saturday with this furry crew. Now that the dust had settled after discovering Rebecca's killers, it felt good to be doing something positive. At least the cats didn't ask how I was every five minutes.

Ethan had moved out of the cabin next door the day before, and I wasn't sure how I felt about it. Now that the case was solved, there was little reason for him to stay at the resort. I looked over my shoulder to check before turning and startled as the ends of my hair brushed my shoulder.

Charlie, true to her word, took me to her cabin after leaving the gym and we'd chopped off my hair. Even though my long hair had become part of my identity, after wearing it that way for most of my life, it felt incredibly freeing to see that huge braid separate from my body. I ran my fingers through it, marveling at how light my head felt. I hadn't worn my hair this short since I'd been in middle-school.

I found a spot in the small parking lot of the park and cut the engine again. I spun around to look at Dex, and found him staring out the window, face intent.

"Is this the one?"

"Maybe?" he said, turning back to me. "Can I get out?"

I glanced at Jasper and he seemed to pick up on my fear. He

cleared his throat and stood on his hind legs so he could see over the seat.

"If it's not, will you come back to the car with us?" he asked. "I know you're feeling itchy. I am, too. I'm not used to riding around in a car, but Eden wants to help this girl. If you run off, we can't do that."

Dex's wary look didn't change, but he nodded slowly and took a deep breath.

"I'll come back."

Willow's eyes were wide as I got out and opened the back door for them. I looked around and breathed a sigh of relief that the park was mostly empty. I fully realized how odd it was to travel around with three cats, not in carriers.

"You know, people do this with dogs all the time," Dex said as he hopped out and sniffed the grass. "I used to see it all the time when I lived in town. I'd hide out near those trees over there when they'd take them off their string things."

He straightened and looked at the trees before glancing at me over his shoulder. I nodded, and he trotted off, tail held high with purpose. He had a point. People didn't think twice about driving around with a dog in their car. Why not cats? Maybe they just needed to be given a chance to travel more.

Willow watched Dex for a moment before tilting her head up to meet my eyes.

"I don't like it. Once we're back home, if I never get in a car again, it will be too soon. I just prefer my paws on the ground."

"You get used to it. I think he found something."

Jasper perked up as Dex lashed his tail back and forth, and the two cats trotted off to meet him. I followed, hands in my pockets against the cold, and smiled at a woman standing near the playground equipment with her children, staring at us like we'd stepped out of a fairy tale. Maybe we had. I waved and continued on, catching up with them. I'd have to be careful with her watching us.

Taking cats on a field trip was one thing. Doing that while talking out loud to them was entirely another. The last thing I wanted was for someone to call the Valewood police to report a strange lady talking to cats in the park. If our mission succeeded, and we found the little girl, I still needed to figure out how to broach the subject with Ethan to get her the help she needed.

"This is it," Dex said, hopping a little in place. "This is where I used to see her. Her house is that way."

He pointed with his tail and I looked at the rows of houses in the distance. We hadn't ventured this far off the beaten path, and I could see why. Unlike the rest of Valewood, which was chock full of adorable little cottages, this part of town looked rougher. I could see peeling paint and broken windows from here.

"Let's walk. I wouldn't mind stretching my legs a little more."

Jasper led the way towards the other cat. Dex was thrumming with energy as we got closer to the homes. He stopped and went stiff as a little girl walked towards us, head down, as she kicked up the snow in front of her. Suddenly, he was off like a shot, bounding along like a kitten. Even from this distance, I could hear her squeal of delight.

"Dex! You came back!"

The three of us paused as she toppled over in the snow, hugging Dex to her chest. I couldn't believe the rough and tumble tom cat let her handle him like that. I started forward again, approaching slowly. I stopped a little distance away and waved at her, sad to see her eyes were full of suspicion as she looked at me.

"Sorry, lady, is he yours?"

Her little face was dirty, hair hanging raggedly out of a stocking hat that was much too big for her. Her pale pink coat was stained and ripped in places and my heart melted as I knelt next to her in the snow.

"I was going to ask you the same question," I said, smiling. "I'm Eden. This is Jasper and that pretty cat there is Willow. What's your name?"

Jasper surprised me by approaching the little girl and looking up at her with complete trust. She slowly reached her hand out, and he hopped up to bump it. Willow stayed further back, but her eyes were friendly as she watched the little girl.

"I'm Charity. My step-dad calls me Charity Case, even though that's not my last name. I've never seen you before. Are you a fairy princess? You're so pretty."

She couldn't have been older than six, and my heart clenched painfully at her words. He was young enough that a woman walking with three cats seemed magical rather than odd.

"No, Charity, I'm just a regular person. I found Dex recently and I've been searching for his owner."

Her blue eyes widened as she looked down at the purring tom, who didn't seem to want to be separated from her.

"And you found me," she said, as her face fell. "But I can't keep him. I want to. I was gonna hide him in my room and share my suppers with him, but my step-dad found out. He yelled awfully loud and scared Dex away."

Tears traced down her cheeks and my hand automatically reached out to her. She winced away before I could touch her.

"Do you have any other family close by, Charity?"

She nodded and backhanded her tears away.

"My grandma lives over there," she said, pointing off into the distance. "But I never get to see her anymore. I don't know why my step-dad doesn't like her. She's so nice. I used to make cookies with her all the time."

"How about your mom?" I asked, fearing the answer.

She shrugged and looked down at Dex, petting him gently between his ears with a finger.

"She's always so tired. She just stays in her bedroom all the time. She's too busy and I don't like to bother her."

I rapidly recalculated my plans. Initially, our goal was to find the little girl and come up with a way to have Ethan do a wellness check or something, and hope the system helped her. Now, meeting her and hearing what was going on at home, there was no way I was going to let her go back there. Not when she had family so close. I pulled out my phone and typed a quick message to Ethan, praying he was nearby.

"Would you like to see your grandma again?" I asked as I put my phone away. "She sounds nice."

Her little face brightened, and she nodded before looking back over her shoulder.

"I don't know if I should. I don't want to make my step-dad angry. He gets angry really easily and I don't like to get hit."

Rage spiked through my soul, and it was all I could do to keep myself together. I looked towards the park.

"I know I'm a stranger, but do you want to go over there to the park with me? There are other people around."

"You're not a stranger," she said, placing her small hand in mine. "Dex is your friend. He's a wonderful cat."

"Yes he is. Let's walk over there and you can tell me more about yourself. I have a friend coming to meet me there and I'd like you to meet him, too."

"Is he your fairy prince?"

"Not exactly, but I think you'll like him."

She chattered, full of life, as we walked back to the park, making a very unlikely group. The cats kept pace with us and I found a picnic table where we could sit and be visible from the parking lot. I checked my phone and saw Ethan's text. He was coming.

Dex curled into Charity's lap, purring so loudly I could hear him from across the table. Jasper settled on my lap while Willow sat next to me. From her tense posture, she wasn't very comfortable, but I could tell she was very interested in the little girl.

"Are you cold?" I asked.

"No, Dex is so warm. How did you find him?"

"Well, that's a long story. I work at the Valewood Resort. Do you know where that is?"

She shook her head, eyes big, and I launched into my story about the clowder and finding Dex in the woods. She looked down at the cap in her lap and patted him carefully.

"He walked all that way? Dex, you must be so tired."

I looked over her shoulder and saw Ethan walking towards us. As he approached, I realized I'd never seen him outside of work. He'd thrown his department coat over a sweatshirt. His sky-blue eyes met mine, and I nodded towards Charity.

"Charity, this is my friend I was telling you about. Ethan, meet Charity."

His freckled face split into a grin as he sat next to me.

"Hi Charity, it's nice to meet you."

She looked at him, eyes barely meeting his, and looked back at Dex, preoccupied with combing through his tabby fur.

"Hi."

He glanced at me, uncertain. I leaned across the table to get her attention.

"Ethan's a police officer, Charity. You can trust him. I think he'd like to hear more about your home life."

Her eyes darted between us and she puckered her face.

"Step-dad says I shouldn't talk to the police. The last time a cop car showed up, he yelled at the cops and our neighbors. And then once they were gone, he yelled at me."

"Is your step-dad Frank Laps?" Ethan asked, his voice soft.

She nodded, wide-eyed.

"You know him?"

"I've heard of him."

"Charity, do you remember your grandma's address?" I asked, looking meaningfully at Ethan.

She nodded and perked up.

"Back before mom started acting weird, she had me memorize it, just in case. I know it by heart."

"Would you like to see your grandma?" Ethan asked. "I can take you to her. It's not safe for a little girl to be wandering around town by herself."

"I'd love to, but can I bring Dex?"

I committed her grandmother to accepting the cat without a second thought. I had a feeling the woman would be thrilled to see her grandchild safe. It wouldn't matter if an entire herd of cats came with her.

"If Dex doesn't mind, I don't see why not."

I looked at the cat in her lap and he blinked slowly at me. I smiled as I realized he'd found his forever home in the heart of this little girl. I wouldn't let him or Charity down. Somehow, we were going to help these two.

"If you don't mind riding with Ethan, I'll follow and grab a few things Dex and you might need."

Her face blanked with terror as she looked at me.

"You're not gonna go to my house, are you?"

"No, sweetheart. I'll stop at a store."

She relaxed and went back to petting Dex.

"Okay. Let's go."

Dex lept down as Charity got up from the table. She put her hand out trustingly to Ethan and he took it gently, bending over a little so she wouldn't have to reach too high. Dex followed, tail high, as we walked over to Ethan's pickup.

He helped Charity in and got her buckled into the passenger seat, and to give him credit, didn't even blink when Dex hopped in and sat on the little girl's lap.

"Ethan, can you text me the address? It will take me a few minutes to grab some things for both of them."

"Of course."

"She's a fairy princess, Mr. Ethan. Did you know that?"

He turned to smile at Charity before looking back at me.

"I think you might be right."

He closed the door and put his hands on his hips, lips curled into a smile.

"Do I even want to know?"

"No, you probably don't. Thank you for coming, Ethan."

"Since you found her wandering by herself, I can definitely take her somewhere safe. If I know Frank Laps, he won't even realize she's gone for a day or two. He and Charity's mom are known around town as the local drug dealers. We've been trying to catch them for years."

My heart ached as I waved at the little girl behind the window. She deserved better, and I could only hope her grandmother would fight for her. If she wouldn't, I certainly would. Somehow.

"See you in a few minutes."

"You've got it."

He smiled and his hair flopped over his forehead. This time, I didn't restrain myself from brushing it to the side.

"Um, I know it's short notice, but we're having a movie night at the resort tonight. Mr. Marsburg is letting us use the lounge and everyone will be there. Would you like to come? If you're not busy, that is."

I looked at my feet as Jasper curled his tail around my leg, lending me some much needed moral support.

"I'd love to."

A smile stretched across my face and it felt like the sun had come out, even though the day was gray and gloomy. I waved at Charity again and turned to go to my car.

"Hey, Eden?"

I turned back as I opened the door for the cats to hop in.

"Yes?"

"I like your hair. It suits you."

"Thanks."

I gave an awkward head bob before walking around my car to get in. Butterflies swarmed in my stomach as I closed the door and put the key in the ignition. I watched as Ethan pulled away and turned to look at the cats.

"Willow, do you mind tagging along with us while I grab some things for Charity and Dex? I can take you back to the resort first."

"No, I want to see that little girl settled. This is fun."

The tortoiseshell cat hopped into the back seat and curled up, eyes bright as I backed out of our parking space. Jasper got comfy next to me and tucked his tail over his muzzle. I drove towards the strip mall in town where I hoped to find cat and little girl supplies, heart singing. I wasn't sure what prompted me to invite Ethan, but I was glad I'd done it. No more hiding in the shadows for me. I was ready to embrace this new life I'd carved out for myself, and thanks to some very special cats, I'd have plenty of help.

DON'T MISS the next book - A Mountain of Mischief!

Don't Miss The Next Book!

A Mountain of Mischief

The Valewood Resort is busier than ever, thanks to the annual snowmobiling race in town. Eden Brooks and the crew are being run ragged trying to keep up. Just when they think they've got a handle on things, everything starts to go wrong.

Someone begins forging their own trails through the nearby forest, disrupting the clowder, and threatening everyone's sanity, and sleep, during their nightly runs. None of the competitors seem to care until sleds go missing and one of their own ends up dead.

The final competition is looming and fingers are being pointed everywhere. Too many suspects and too many motives mean it's going to take all of Eden's skills to save the clowder and help Ethan Rhodes solve the case.

Have you read The Razzy Cat Cozy Mystery Series?

The Body in the Park
A Razzy Cat Cozy Mystery

"I'm a cat lover and read many cat mysteries. Courtney McFarlin's Razzy Cat Cozy Mystery Series is my favorite."

She's found an unlikely consultant to help solve the crime. But this speaking pet might just prove purr-fect...

Hannah Murphy yearns for a real news story. But after a strange migraine results in an unexpected ability to talk to her cat, she must keep the kitty-communication skills a secret if she wants to advance from fluff pieces to covering felonies. And when she literally trips over a slain body, she's shocked her feline companion is the best partner to crack the case.

Convinced she's finally got her big break, Hannah quickly runs afoul of a handsome detective and his poor opinion of interfering reporters. And when she discovers the victim's penchant for embezzlement and fraud, she may need more than a furry friend and a cantankerous cop to avoid ending up in the obits.

Can Hannah catch a killer before her career and her life are dead and buried?

The Body in the Park is the delightful first book in the Razzy Cat cozy mystery series. If you like clever sleuths, light banter, and talking animals, then you'll love Courtney McFarlin's hilarious whodunit.

More reader comments: "The Razzy Cat series is a joy to read! I have read the first three, and just bought the fourth. These books are well written, engaging stories. I love the positive and supportive relationships depicted amongst the main characters and the cats. That is so refreshing to read. I look forward to more books in this series. I will also be reading some this author's other works. Well done, and keep writing!" - Ingrid

Buy *The Body in the Park* for the long arm of the paw today!

Books By Courtney McFarlin

Escape from Reality Cozy Mystery Series

Escape from Danger

Escape from the Past

Escape from Hiding

A Razzy Cat Cozy Mystery Series

The Body in the Park

The Trouble at City Hall

The Crime at the Lake

The Thief in the Night

The Mess at the Banquet

The Girl Who Disappeared

Tails by the Fireplace

The Love That Was Lost

The Problem at the Picnic

The Chaos at the Campground

The Crisis at the Wedding

The Murder on the Mountain

The Reunion on the Farm

The Mishap at the Meeting

The Bones on the Trail - Coming December 2023

A Soul Seeker Cozy Mystery

The Apparition in the Attic

The Banshee in the Bathroom

The Creature in the Cabin

The ABCs of Seeing Ghosts

The Demon in the Den

The Ether in the Entryway

The Fright in the Family Room

The Ghoul in the Garage

The Haunting in the Hallway

The Imp at the Ice Rink

The Jinn in the Joists

The Kelpie in the Kennel - Coming 2024!

The Clowder Cats Cozy Mystery Series

Resorting to Murder

A Slippery Slope

A Mountain of Mischief - Coming in the Spring of 2024!

A Note From Courtney

Thank you for taking the time to read this novel. If you enjoyed the book, please take a few minutes to leave a review. As an independent author, I appreciate the help!

If you'd like to be first in line to hear about new books as they are released, don't forget to sign up for my newsletter. Click here to sign up! https://bit.ly/2H8BSef

A Little About Me

Courtney McFarlin currently lives in the Black Hills of South Dakota with her fiancé and their two cats.

Find out more about her books at:
www.booksbycourtney.com

Follow Courtney on Social Media:

https://twitter.com/booksbycourtney

https://www.instagram.com/courtneymcfarlin/

https://www.facebook.com/booksbycourtneym

Made in the USA
Monee, IL
14 November 2024